A KISS FOR CARTER

SOMETIMES LOVE IS A TALL STORY

DAVINA STONE

Ebook ISBN: 978-0-6450065-4-4

Print ISBN: 978-0-6450065-5-1

Cover design by Bailey McGinn, Bailey Designs Books

Edited by Vanessa Lanaway, Red Dot Scribble

*This book is dedicated to
anyone who once sat
alone in the playground.*

*A Kiss for Carter is set in a Covid-free parallel universe. Please relax and
enjoy!*

PLAY LIST

- *Walking On Sunshine*—Katrina and The Waves.
- *Gold*—Spandau Ballet.
- *Baby I Love You*—The Ramones.
- *Tainted Love*—Soft Cell
- *Sexual Healing*—Marvin Gaye
- *Relax (don't do it)*—Frankie Goes to Hollywood.
- *Vienna,*—Ultravox.
- *Like A Virgin*—Madonna
- *Manic Monday*—The Bangles
- *Money For Nothing*—Dire Straits
- *Fields of Gold*—Sting
- *I'm Gonna Be (Walk 500 miles)*—The Proclaimers.
- *It Must have Been Love*—Roxette.
- *Up Where We Belong*—Jennifer Warnes/Joe Cocker
- *Imagine*—John Lennon
- *L'Apres midi d'un faune*—Claude Debussy
- *Concerto for Flute and Harp in C Major*—Mozart
- *Flute Sonata in B-Flat Major, K. 10, Op. 3 No. 1: I. Allegro*
  —Mozart

CHAPTER 1

*T*he guy in the menswear department eyed Carts' ankles with a polite smile.

Carts was used to it, the slightly pitying look that said, "these are the longest pants we stock, dude".

He'd already sussed the guy out as one of those trendy buffed nuggets who probably spent all his free time pumping iron. His slicked back, product-filled hair topped a head that barely skimmed Carts' shoulder. What he lacked in height he certainly made up for in muscle.

The guy— Baz, he'd introduced himself as—stepped back, crossed his arms and rubbed the designer stubble on his chin. Carts wished he hadn't grabbed the first threadbare pair of socks he'd found in his drawer this morning.

Baz narrowed his eyes. Which did nothing to help the situation.

Tomorrow. The thought made his heart sputter behind his ribs. By tomorrow evening he had to be spruced to the max. And that meant pant hems that didn't flap around the ends of his calf bones, and no wrists showing below his cuffs.

Baz wagged an enthusiastic finger in the air. "I think I may have a suit in the back with extra leg length."

Carts peered out from under his fringe. "Designer brand?"

"Of course, mate, of course. I hear you." Baz tugged at his earlobe. Carts stifled a sigh. Buying clothes when you were 6'6" (and a half) was sheer hell. Not only the change rooms, which near enough exposed your nipples over the top of the curtain, but the pitying looks, the suggestions that maybe if he wore a pair of boots instead of shoes the hem discrepancy wouldn't show. And as for the jacket. "Buy yourself a pair of trendy cufflinks" a nice motherly woman had said once, "that'll draw attention away from the shortfall in the sleeves, love."

Sometimes it felt like the whole menswear industry of Perth saw him coming and had their lines rehearsed. Which was a dumb-arsed thought, because up until two weeks ago he only went clothes shopping when absolutely essential, which added up to twice a year at most.

By now, Baz had sped off to the stock cupboard and Carts flicked a look at his phone. His shoulders sagged. No message from Polly.

He'd sent her an urgent text to let her know he was shopping for suits and needed her advice. No reply. Since his thirtieth birthday party last Saturday Polly had gone to ground. It didn't make sense; she'd been so helpful the week before, helping him decide which shirt to buy to impress Judith. Carts sighed and pocketed his phone. Even though he'd known her since uni, sometimes sussing out Polly's moods was like trying to find a golf ball in a blizzard.

Then he thought about Judith, and his heart fluttered like it had grown wings. Judith. Wow! He was smitten, wasn't he? Every time he thought of her his insides melted like gooey caramel.

He'd kissed her.

She'd kissed him back.

In the dim light of the street after all the other guests had left and the moon hung like a golden crescent backlit by a zillion southern hemisphere stars, he'd freakin' kissed her. He was a born romantic, so of course he'd noticed the sky show. And when he'd circled her tentatively with his arms and pointed out the Southern Cross, Judith's eyes had shone like the two most radiant stars of all.

He'd bitten his lip and swallowed the words that formed on his tongue. He'd told women things like that before only to get kicked in

Quickly she tugged off her work blouse and skirt and shimmied into the first dress. Smoothed it down her legs, swivelled this way, then that, and flicked her long blonde hair out around her shoulders.

Pouted at her reflection.

Then slapped a hand over her mouth. Her eyes creased mischievously over the top of her fingers.

Really, she wasn't prone to pouting, but it felt kind of fun. Out of character, but fun.

Because since Carts' kiss she'd felt different. Like suddenly she was visible. In the romantic sense—even—deep breath in, the *sexual* sense. She'd always felt visible as the good girl, the girl who studied to be an occupational therapist and put her family and boyfriend first. She thought of all the times she'd taken Mark's dinner to him while he was gaming on his computer. Bought his favourite chocolate to bribe him into sitting with her on a Saturday night to watch a Netflix show. Not to mention the hours spent working in her craft room on some intricate project, pretending that this was how it should be. Comfortable. Like a pair of old slippers when really, like Polly, she should be out dancing in a pair of Jimmy Choos.

Now, on to the next dress...

Fifteen minutes later she was at the counter with three dresses over her arm, because she was darned well going to spend her holiday funds on clothes if she felt like it!

Her planned holiday with Mark had fizzled when he announced he was leaving her. She'd saved six thousand dollars towards air fares and accommodation. In the name of fairness, she'd handed half of that to Mark, but there was still three thousand dollars in her savings account, doing nothing except gaining a dribble of interest.

She placed the dresses on the counter and drew out her purse, handed over her debit card to the girl with barely a qualm. She'd always been cautious, but now, to hell with that. She was going to splurge on clothes and... who knew what next? A new sofa maybe, just so she didn't have to remember Mark sitting there munching through Cadbury's fruit and nut, shoulders stooped and chin jutting as he stared at the TV.

"It didn't go through." The store assistant's voice cut through her musings. Judith blinked. The woman was holding the card up like it was a court summons.

"Oh—no, there must be some mistake."

"I'll try it again, could be our system." Judith watched the woman's red shellacked nails as she tapped at the keypad, waved the card over the screen. Beep. Declined.

This could not be happening.

"Maybe your card's damaged." The woman had a condescending look in her eyes. Judith sensed herself blushing and mustered, "Could you try one more time? There's plenty of funds in that account."

The assistant's lip curled. "Sure."

Judith waited, her fingers drilling a nervous tattoo on the service desk.

Beep.

"Would you like to use another payment method?" The woman handed Judith the card.

Blushing furiously now, Judith flicked through the cards in her purse. She didn't like using her credit card too often, though she always paid it off each month to avoid accruing fees. Mark never had a clue about finances and always overspent, and each time, they'd had to do a major reckoning and eat sausages and mash for a week until their next pay came through.

She handed over her credit card and sighed with relief when it all went through fine.

As she left the shop, a little frown knotted her forehead.

There were three thousand dollars sitting in her savings account.

She knew her PIN off by heart.

So why hadn't the payment gone through?

CHAPTER 2

 hen Carts arrived at his parents' home, the kid who'd been torturing the piano was leaving. Even from a distance he could see Mum had her teaching face on, nodding and smiling, though he knew all she wanted was for the helicopter parent to take her daughter and go hover over her at netball or tennis or whatever class she had next.

He could see dark rings under the kid's eyes even from the footpath.

As the woman and her daughter got into their car, Carts headed up the path.

Mum's mouth tilted into a relieved smile at the sight of him, but the furrow between her eyebrows remained. He hugged her hard. Rosemary Wells was on the up-side of six foot, but she seemed small and fragile in his arms.

She ushered him inside and shut the door.

"Where is she?" he asked, shrugging off his jacket.

"In her room with the door barricaded."

"You've locked her in!"

His mum sighed. "No, love, she's locked *me* out."

"Fuck!"

"Carter, can you please not swear."

"Sorry. So, what's happened this time?"

This time was getting to be the standard phrase with regard to Avery. Not even a year ago, Avery had been a model kid—studious, quiet, dedicated to her music and intent on getting a scholarship to the Conservatorium in Paris.

Then something changed. She became sullen. She avoided eye contact. Grunted at Mum and Dad. Even grunted at him. Like, *what?* Avery had always adored him. He'd been fourteen when she was born and he remembered holding the tiny bundle in his arms, marvelling at those teeny-weeny fingers, her crumpled, plum-coloured newborn face with all that dark fuzz on top of her head. He'd been totally smitten ever since.

And up until a month ago she'd adored him too. As she grew from a baby to a toddler, her nappy hanging low on chubby legs, Avery had followed him around the house like his shadow. He was there when she started Kindy, and for her first day of primary school. Had watched with pride as she received the music prize each year, and attended each and every one of her concerts.

"You need to talk some sense into her," Mum said, as Carts strode into the music room and flung his jacket on the old leather sofa.

"I need the full story first."

Mum busied herself tidying music sheets. "She's—" stopping abruptly, she pinched the bridge of her nose. Was she about to cry? After a second, to his relief, she dropped her hand and continued to sort papers. "She's saying she won't take the scholarship if she gets it."

"Where's this suddenly come from?"

"We had a fight."

"What about?"

Mum closed the piano lid with a thud. "Oh, some party she wants to go to next weekend. That awful girl Zany—or Zammy or whatever her name is. You know the one, with skirts that practically show off her knickers."

"Urm—" He didn't. He'd occasionally dropped Avery at school, but he wouldn't be able to tell one kid in uniform from another. Unless they had purple hair or something.

"She's the one who dyed her hair purple," Mum supplied.

"Oh, yeah, right." Now he recalled a conversation at dinner a couple of weeks ago, about Avery wanting to put silver streaks in her hair because her friend had dyed hers. Goodness, me, Mum had said, you'll be old before you can blink, why on earth do you want to speed the process up? Dad had muttered his standard line of listen to your mother, then focused on cutting up his lamb chop.

A sudden bass beat raised both their gazes to the ceiling. Mum shook her head and pursed her lips. "See! This is what I have to put up with every day after school."

Carts' ears pricked. "Triple J radio."

"Sounds like a cat fight to me," Mum grumbled.

"What does Dad say?"

"I'm trying not to bring him into it. What with his interview last week for the new head of department role—he's very stressed about the restructure."

Carts sighed. He wanted to get home and try on his new suit again and work out whether to wear Baz's tie. If so, should he keep it on, or take it off just after he'd met her? He rather liked the idea of tugging it off, pocketing it casually, then flipping open his shirt collar, maybe even seeing Judith's gaze linger on his neck for a moment.

He needed to practise his moves in the mirror.

"I'll go up and see if she'll talk to me," he said, patting Mum on the arm before taking the stairs two at a time.

As he got closer, the *thump, thump, doof-doof* practically made the door vibrate. He tapped lightly.

No response.

He tried again, rapping harder with his knuckles.

"Avery. Av-ery it's me." Louder, "Open up for your brother, will you?"

Nothing.

"C'mon Aves." Wheedling was not the easiest over heavy metal.

Carts leaned his forehead against the door, just as it swung open and he catapulted into Avery's room like a human shotput.

"WhatdyouWANT?" Avery shouted as Carts practically bounced off the far wall and she bounced onto the bed.

"What sort of greeting is that?" Carts shouted back as he regained his balance, and tried to lean nonchalantly against the wall. "Can you turn that off?"

Avery hugged her knees to her chest and scowled at him, then reluctantly reached for her phone. Carts' ears gave thanks for the blessed silence that ensued.

"You're so unco," Avery muttered.

"Thanks." He popped his eyes at her. "*Hullo, big brother,* how nice of you to come and see me."

Her chin dipped lower, but he caught a smirk hovering on her lips. Though, now he was looking at her properly, something was weird with her eyes. He pushed off the wall and squinted at her face. "What have you done to your eyes?"

"It's kohl."

"Yeah, looks like you've been down a coal mine, that's for sure."

"Not coal, you tool, kohl. K-O-H-L."

Carts waggled his eyebrows. "The ghoul next door look."

"Haha, very funny. It's goth. Guess you wouldn't know what that is either, you're so ancient."

"For your info, goth has been a thing longer than you've been alive." Carts pulled a face at her. "I nearly dated a goth once."

"Yeah, right." Avery's lip curled, not buying a word of it. "Has Mum sent you up here?"

He moved over and sat on the bed, rubbed her foot. Her toes were cold, they'd always been cold even as a little girl. Her toenails, he noticed with a jolt, were painted black.

"Maybe." No point in lying, sixteen-year-olds had an antennae for fibs. He rubbed her toes and she curled them away. "Don't."

"Your feet are like icicles. Why aren't you wearing your Uggs?"

"In case my nails aren't dry."

"Show me your fingers."

She splayed her long fingers out. The nails were thankfully bare. "Mum would just make me take it off, not worth wasting time doing them."

They sat quietly for a few moments, Carts still stroking her ankle, and working out his strategy. In the end he figured the no-bullshit approach was best.

"So, what's the story? About the flute?"

Avery's chin rubbed from one kneecap to the other, her eyes accentuated by the kohl, huge and the same velvet brown as his own. "It's a revenge tactic."

"For what."

"For mum not letting me go to Zammy's party next week."

"You're not really serious about giving up your music?"

"I will if she doesn't let me go."

"Oh, Aves, this is silly."

She glared. "Why?"

"It's so short-sighted. Think about what you've achieved. How amazingly freakin' talented you are. If I had a teaspoon of your talent, I'd—"

"You'd what, fart-face?"

Oh, she really had a knack right now, did Avery. He thinned his lips. All he'd ever shown was an aptitude for numbers. Which meant he'd followed the career counsellor's advice and become an accountant. Not even thought to question it. Unimaginative. Dull. Predictable. And here was his shining star of a sister about to throw away her brilliance. Hit the ground like a meteorite.

"Never mind," he said. "I'm past being able to make changes. But you, Aves, you have your whole life ahead of you. A career that could take you all over the world. A scholarship opportunity to study in Paris."

"Don't want to."

"Why the fuck not?"

"Oooh, I'll tell Mum. She'll make you put money in the swear jar."

"Why wouldn't you want to go to Paris?"

"I can't speak French."

"You'll learn."

"They eat frogs. And snails. That's weird. I'd barf if I tried to eat that stuff."

"No-one will make you eat frogs or snails. Is that all?"

13

Silence, then barely audible, "They won't like me."

In a flash Carts' arms were around her and her head rocked against his chest. A big hiccup of a sob tore at his heart. "They don't like me here so why would they like me there?"

"Oh, Aves."

"Only Zammy likes me. That's why I have to go to her party. Everyone else hates me." She tunnelled deeper into him, her words muffled. "You know what they call me at school?" She looked up briefly, tragic-eyed. "Budgie."

He gave her a perplexed look and she added in an exasperated tone, "*Av-er-y*. Get it? Why did Mum and Dad have to call me that stupid name?"

A shot of pure rage hit Carts between the ribs. How dare the little shites say those things? "It's a great name."

"It's not," she buried back into his shirt.

"I used to get called Stick Insect. At least you're one up the pecking order. Get it? *Pecking order.*"

Avery groaned loudly, "Your jokes are so bad." The snuffle turned to a sniff then something that might be construed as a giggle. "And Mum and Dad's taste in names is up their arse."

"Swear jar." He squeezed her tight.

"Fuck off." She squeezed back. When she pulled away, he looked down at the great damp patch on his shirt from her tears and snot and two great big black blotches of kohl. "The things I do for you, this is my best shirt."

"Then your tastes up your arse too."

Now they were both laughing. "I got a new suit today," he said, relieved the mood had lightened.

"Really, why?" She was swiping at her nostrils with the back of her hand. Carts got up and found a tissue box among the debris of make-up on her dressing table and handed it to her. Avery pulled out reams and scrubbed at her nose and eyes. He guessed it would be good to let her focus on his news while she put herself back together. Then he'd revisit the flute problem.

"Maybe I've got a hot date." A telltale heat crept up his neck.

CHAPTER 3

*J*udith typed the account password into her laptop, a pulse pounding at her temples as she stared at the screen.

Her eyes scanned the account details.

Balance: zero. She blinked hard. Looked again. Still zero.

Fingers of ice crawled across her scalp and down her spine. This could not be happening.

Her three thousand dollars was gone. The money she'd squirrelled away from her pay packet each month, feeling empowered that she was saving towards their overseas holiday. Gone.

Fingers shaking, she pulled up the details of the account.

Her eyes widened at the last entry. Three withdrawals of nine hundred dollars, on three consecutive days, which was the limit she'd put on account withdrawals.

Oh, and a neat little thirty dollars to round it all off on day four.

All paid into the account of one Mark Downing.

Now the tight, icy feeling had spread to her chest, like poison ivy threatening to squeeze the breath out of her lungs.

Why would Mark do this? She'd paid him his share; it had never occurred to her she would need to close off that account.

And now, without asking, he'd taken what wasn't his.

Her forehead was so tight she was worried her skull might crack with the pressure.

There must be some explanation. She scrubbed two fingers across the crease that had formed between her eyebrows, as though if she got rid of it, this would all magically go away. She racked her brains. Maybe his salary hadn't come through this month, or he'd had to pay some extra bills. No, that didn't make sense. He'd had enough for the bond and two months' rent payments. They'd organised all that.

Sure, Mark had fallen out of love with her, but that didn't make him a *bad* person.

It didn't make him someone who would *steal* from her.

She stood up so abruptly her chair clattered to the floor. Hugging herself, she paced the kitchen, rubbing the tops of her arms, which were numb with shock.

Finally, she grabbed her phone off the island bench and brought up Mark's number. Typed in, *Have you stolen my money?*

Erased it. She hated sounding accusatory, there had to be some more logical explanation. *Mark, we have to talk.*

That would have to do. She pressed send.

Then followed it with *URGENT.*

Before the split, he'd been good at phoning her, admittedly more often than not to check if she'd bought chocolate on her way home from work. She hadn't heard much since he'd moved out. Truthfully, she was worried she'd go around to his apartment and find him dead from gaming. She'd heard that could happen on a talkback show about problem gaming. She'd recognised the classic signs in Mark. People just sat at their computers, so immersed that they forgot to eat, forgot to drink, forgot to pee. And then their hearts stopped. They simply dropped dead in the middle of slaying dragons or demons or whatever.

The minutes ticked by loudly on the clock above the stove.

Finally, she couldn't stand it any longer and called him.

No answer. He'd taken off his voice message. That was strange.

She tried again, tapping in his number manually even though it had always gone through on automatic dial before.

Still no answer.

them out and put them on hangers, then laid them neatly side by side on her bed.

She wasn't going to think about the money right now.

On reflection, the mint green one was her favourite. But it did need work around the top. She often had to alter dresses due to the fact that her right breast was a cup size bigger than the other. It was a fact she'd come to terms with. Mostly. Except... she hadn't shown her breasts to a man, other than Mark, ever.

Mark had been it, as far as sex went. Unless you counted a grope in the sand dunes with a guy when she was barely sixteen. She'd only let him touch one of her breasts, the bigger one.

What if... The tingle in her cheeks intensified. Oh, no, not yet. Not for a long while. She'd go slow, very, very slow.

Besides, how did you really know you could trust someone? She'd trusted Mark, and suddenly out of the blue he'd upped and left. Not a single sign, or at least none that she'd recognised. The money issue scooted into her head again and her stomach turned into a tight, hard ball of tension. She decided to face it when she'd calmed down. Trying to tackle problems when you were riled up never solved anything. She'd watched Pippa do that with Mum and it never, ever worked.

Nope. She scooped up the mint green dress and headed for her craft room.

Right now, she was going to get out her sewing machine and make that dress fit like a dream.

CHAPTER 4

"*W*ells!"

Tiptoeing past Ron Towers' office, Carts froze.

The door was only open a crack, how the heck did Ron know it was him? Some kind of chemical reaction as he walked past? Photosynthesis, like plants? He'd started a book last night on the language of trees in an attempt to keep his mind off his date with Judith. Because one infinitesimal thought of her, and his body was at risk of some very serious chemical reactions of its own.

"Come in here," Ron bellowed.

Carts sighed and nudged the door open with his foot. "Yes, Ron."

Ron's bulbous eyes pinned him, glasses on the end of his nose. A pudgy hand waved in the air. "I'm over here, boy."

"Yes, Ron, I can see you." *Unfortunately.*

"Ah, so there *is* a pair of eyes under that thatch."

Carts gritted his teeth until his jaw felt like it would crack.

He'd actually tried to get a haircut at lunch time, after he'd had no luck with his phone screen repair. "Have it back to you next week, mate," the dude in the arcade had said with a shrug. So, he'd kept his smashed phone for now and walked two doors down to The Right Cut. A woman with blonde hair tied into a messy ponytail wearing a T-shirt with "HAIR VIP" scrawled over the front in glitter, called out, "Hullo, there."

Carts could only stare in confusion. "Where's Bernie?"

He'd been coming to Bernie since he'd started working at Pearson's Accounting eight years ago. Bernie got his hair. Never insisted on cutting off too much.

"Bernie's retired." He watched as the woman did something weird with foil on her client's head. "I've taken over the business. We're unisex now."

Carts had to struggle not to recoil.

"I'm Tara." The woman advanced, pinging off her rubber gloves. "I could do you while the colour sets on my client. Haven't got time for a full wash and blow-dry, but if you don't mind me cutting you dry..." She chortled; a sound that put the fear of God into him.

'Maybe I'll come back later," he managed.

Tara shrugged. "Okay, darlin', open till 8 pm. I do walk-ins. But there might be a wait." She cocked her head and her eyes narrowed. "Sure you don't want to go for it now?"

"No! Thanks. Are you open tomorrow?"

"Here until midday. Got my kids' sport in the arvo."

"Okay. Morning it is then." Grinning like a hyena, Carts backed rapidly out the door.

Bernie retired? Bernie was an icon in the city with his barber's pole and his habit of grunting and smelling of cigarette smoke and whisky. He hadn't said a word last time Carts came for a trim. Mind you, last time *had* been three months ago. And Bernie barely spoke anyway.

In a bit of a daze, he'd gone to Myer and bought a pair of scissors, but every time he sneaked into the men's bathroom at work, intent on trimming a fraction off his fringe, someone would burst through the door.

Travis Green, the office loudmouth, had spied the scissors before Carts could whisk them behind his back and snickered. "Working here that bad, is it?"

Now it would be all round the office that Carter Wells was doing weird shit with a pair of scissors in the men's loos.

So he gave up, reassuring himself that grunge in a suit was "in" and battled through his workload for the rest of the afternoon.

But now, standing in front of Ron's desk, the bolstering of his ego fizzled. Of course, Ron wouldn't think to mention Carts' beautifully cut suit. Or his sea blue tie with embroidered silver shells on it. Oh no, Ron loved to accentuate the negative. That was the trouble with men in their late fifties who hadn't made it past middle management. Bitter and twisted. As if the only power they had to wield was making the world a more mean-spirited place.

Carts raised himself up to his full height. "Did you want me for anything in particular, Ron?"

"Yes. I was just sending you an email. I'm taking some leave from Monday. I need you to cover my clients."

Carts frowned. "Monday? I didn't know you were planning a holiday."

Ron scrubbed a hand through his thinning hair. "Yeah, well, decided I needed a break. Work my backside off for Pearson's, and what do they do for me in return, eh?"

Carts didn't say a word; everyone knew Ron milked the Pearson cow, had done for years. Ron glanced up and growled. "Don't look at me like I've lost my bloody marbles. I don't like having to do this, my clients aren't overjoyed at being passed over to you, but you're the most experienced I've got. I've told them not to expect great things. But they get that the boss needs a break from time to time."

"You'll leave me some instructions?"

"Ah, Jesus, you'll work it out. It's hardly rocket science."

There it was, his workload was going to triple next week. A host of frustrated small business owners expecting him to fix up the fact they'd kept three years of receipts in a shoebox and now the tax office was breathing down their neck. Somehow he'd cope. He always did. Ron might bend him, but he sure as fuck would not break him. "Not a problem. Anything else, Ron?"

"Calling it a day already, are we?" Ron made a big deal of looking at his watch. "Off to that weird woo-woo stuff you get up to on a Friday?"

"No, not tonight." He'd made the mistake a few months back of telling Travis he did yoga and it had spread like wildfire round the office.

Ron gave a snort of derision and returned to his computer screen. "Go on then, scarper." Carts made for the door, "Oi, one more thing—"

Fingers gripping the doorknob, he muttered, "Yes, Ron." He knew what was coming.

"Get a bloody haircut."

Carts shut the door just hard enough to send a clear message.

Not that the old sod would notice.

On the street he tried to breathe out the tension from his exchange with Ron and checked his phone. There was a text from Dan, distorted by his crazy-paving screen.

Stop being a soft cock and come to the pub.

Carts grinned. Since Aaron had left for an extended trip to Europe with Alice, and Carts had taken up yoga, the third member of their trio, Dan, regularly grumbled that the Friday night drinking tradition had ground to a halt. Despite his complaints, Carts knew Dan was happy enough to scull pints of Guinness and talk tackles with the guys from his rugby team.

He contemplated a response along the lines of a hard cock, but immediately thought better of it. That would be disrespectful to Judith.

He was thirty. Time to man up.

He might even put his own swear jar in the kitchen at home; when he had kids, he wouldn't want them to be lisping out bad language at kindy, would he?

A sudden warm glow spread through his chest. He'd never hidden the fact he'd love to have kids in the not-too-distant future. That he wanted to marry and settle down. He had the house, but it needed a woman's touch. And you could bet Judith's would be tasteful. His eyes must have gone kind of dreamy because when his phone pinged with another message he had to blink to focus on the cracked screen.

It was from Mum: *I've decided to let Avery go. As long as you take her and pick her up at 10 sharp.*

He sent a thumbs-up emoji.

A win. So why did he feel vaguely queasy? Had he done the right thing? After his talk with Avery yesterday, he'd spent an hour persuading Mum that it was a good idea to let her go to the party. That it was important for a girl of sixteen to fit in, to be part of the group. That giving a little would result in a gain in the long run. He'd reassured Mum that Avery still loved the flute and it was just a hang-up about French food. Mum had looked sceptical. "She didn't mind eating a witchetty grub at the science expo your dad put on at her school."

Carts shrugged. "Bravado. Probably showing off to her mates that her dad's a big wig science lecturer."

Mum grunted. Her onion chopping got fiercer. "Do you want to stay for dinner?"

"Not tonight. Got a big day tomorrow."

Mum cast him a dark look. "When are you going to get another job? That man's a slave driver."

"He's okay," Carts said, avoiding her eyes while shunting on his jacket. She didn't believe a word, of course, but he wanted to strut his stuff in front of the mirror, not get into another discussion about his self-worth.

When he kissed her goodbye, she'd grudgingly said she'd think about the party issue.

And now it had come down in Avery's favour. She owed him big time.

He checked his phone once more. No message from Judith, so presumably she wasn't running late or standing him up.

Then he messaged Dan back.

Shanti, dude. Shanti.

A bit of yoga speak would surely get up Dan's nose.

Not wanting to be early, he slowed his pace and regretted leaving his briefcase at work, because now he didn't know what to do with his hands. He shoved them nonchalantly into his pants pockets and sauntered towards the river. He'd organised a fantastic restaurant on Elizabeth Quay. Spent a couple of lunch breaks this week checking the options out before booking, ensuring he found one with the right ambient lighting and seating arrangements, not to mention polite service. The woman who took his reservation had been delightful. These things mattered when you were courting.

Courting. Jeesh, that sounded like a line out of one of the old-fashioned novels Alice used to read. And then he realised something. He wasn't sad, he wasn't envious.

About Alice choosing Aaron over him.

Because if she hadn't, he would never have met Judith.

SHE SAW HIM FIRST. You couldn't miss the dark head bobbing several inches above the crowds on the busy Friday night precinct.

She had the opportunity to study him before he spotted her. Sharp cheekbones, an expressive mouth, currently a little tight-lipped, his angular jaw made more rugged by a shadow of a beard. She liked the way he wore his hair almost touching his collar, how it hung rakishly over his eyes. It offset the fact that those eyes were officially the gentlest she'd ever seen. And a touch sad. If his hair was shorter, he'd look almost too vulnerable, like a lost boy out of Peter Pan.

Suddenly he spotted her, quickly sweeping back his fringe with the back of his hand, and a little zing of heat swirled into her belly as those eyes lit up and his mouth shaped into a heart-stopping smile.

When he got up close, she could really admire how much effort he'd made.

"I love your tie." She stared hard at the shell pattern as shyness threatened to overwhelm her.

When her eyes flicked back to his face, the smile had turned gorgeously goofy and his cheeks were flushed. "Thanks. If I may say so, that's a very pretty dress."

"Oh, you like it?"

"I do. Give me a twirl. Er, if you like twirling, of course."

Judith laughed. "I'll twirl for you if you twirl for me."

"Done."

He tucked his chin with a smirk and did a 360-degree turn, hands dug deep in his pockets. His shoulders looked fantastic in that jacket, she thought. When he turned to face her again his eyebrows lifted into his hairline in a way that made her giggle.

"Score out of ten?" he asked.

"Definitely a ten."

"Your turn now."

She shimmied her hips awkwardly, then twizzled on the spot, slightly lost her footing, and faced him again, feeling utterly stupid.

But Carts was gazing at her so warmly that the feeling vanished, leaving nothing but the thud of her heart and a honeyed warmth thrumming in a place so long forgotten she'd thought it had grown over with briars and moss. "That's a twelve," he said.

"Twelve!"

"Yep. Twelve out of ten."

She laughed and Carts added, "The thing about being an accountant is you can break the rules."

"Well, I'll happily take a twelve from the expert. It's new," she said, brushing nervous hands down the folds of her skirt. "I bought it yesterday."

"Me too. The suit. And the tie. To be honest, the tie was a gift. From Baz."

"Baz?"

"The guy I bought the suit off. He threw in the tie." His sharp bark of a laugh told her he was as nervous as she was. "Not that I was buying a new suit for any *particular* reason, of course."

She cast what she hoped came over as a flirtatious glance from under her lashes, saw him draw in a breath and knew she'd hit the mark. "Are you sure about that?" she asked, and wow, did her voice come out low and sultry.

Carts gave a little cough and adjusted his tie. Her gaze sprang to his throat and his Adam's apple bobbed. "I think on that note we should probably go and grab our table," he said huskily.

As he stood back to let her go first, his height made her feel safe, and… petite. Mark was several centimetres shorter than her and it had always been a bone of contention. He'd insisted on her wearing flats, otherwise he said he felt like a kid out with his mum.

The memory brought on the familiar droop to her spine. She straightened, but try as she might, she couldn't quite get that sultry vibe back. Luckily a waiter swooped and showed them to their table.

Judith sat down, put her bag on the floor, flicked her hair around her shoulders and found herself playing with a strand. Oh god, why couldn't she just be calm and sophisticated? She tethered her hands tightly in her lap.

By now Carts had removed his jacket and placed it carefully on the chair back and sat down opposite her. An awkward silence ensued while the waiter shook out their napkins, placed them on their laps, and then left them with the drinks menu.

Carts frowned as his eye travelled up and down the page.

"Do you prefer red or white?" He shot her a slightly panicked look. "Or we could go for a rosé… or even a sparkling?"

"How about we get a bottle of the house white?" she suggested, and his face immediately relaxed.

"Easy-peasy," he agreed, and placed an arm on the table. His elbow knocked his water glass and he grabbed it quickly to stop it upending. Judith's heart went out to him; long arms and small tables, she knew from personal experience, were a bad combination.

When the waiter had taken their order and left, she drew in a deep breath.

Carts did the same.

"How was your day?" they both said in unison.

AFTER THE FIRST course Carts could feel his nervous system dialling down from flame-grilled to nicely marinated. Nothing at all to do with his twice-cooked lamb shank, excellent though it was, and everything to do with basking in Judith's attention.

After those awkward first moments, they'd talked with relative ease. If there was a brief moment of silence, Judith would say something, and he'd look at her and shake his head and say, "Oh my god, I was just about to ask *you* that."

He'd even managed to remove his tie, flip open the top two buttons of his shirt and bask in the glorious feeling of Judith's gaze roaming to his neck. When he'd glanced at her she'd flicked her eyes away quickly. But he'd seen it, and it felt like a warm hug around his heart.

By dessert they'd worked through why they'd chosen their careers— briefly, on his part, because he knew he was prone to yabbering on about himself. Besides, what was remotely interesting about choosing to be an accountant? Instead, he'd let Judith talk about how her love of people and the arts had combined in her dream job as an occupational therapist. And now they were onto siblings.

"So, I'm the oldest, Luke's the middle child and then Pippa's the youngest. She was a kind of afterthought. And she's really different from the rest of us."

"In what way?"

"Rambunctious, I'd describe her as."

"Good word. What's it mean exactly?" English never had been his strong suit at school.

"I guess like it sounds. Energetic. Boisterous."

"Not at all like you then." He softened his tone, gazed deeply into her eyes. Until a sliver of hair fell across his vision, and he had to flick it out of the way.

"Should I take that as a compliment?" Judith asked, toying with a piece of chicken.

"Absolutely."

She looked down, her cheeks pink. He hoped he wasn't being too forward with the compliments; it would be awful to come over as a sleaze. Frankly, this whole dating business was a minefield of possible wrong moves.

"Avery is a lot younger than you, isn't she?" Judith said, smiling in a way that was definitely encouraging. Nevertheless, he was relieved at the subject change. He'd told Judith proudly about Avery's music talent at one of their after-yoga chats a couple of weeks ago. Of course, he'd wanted to impress someone as artistic as Judith, but also, he was seri-ously proud of his little sis.

"Yes, there's fourteen years between us. Mum had some fertility problems, hence the big age gap. She's sixteen." He thought about the party problem and sighed.

"Is something the matter?" Judith asked. Perceptive or what?

"Oh just… things aren't the best with her right now."

"Oh dear, why not?"

"Teenage stuff. Giving my parents a bit of grief, that's all."

"Can I ask why?" She was leaning her chin in her hands, her eyes full of genuine concern, and despite vowing he wasn't going to talk too much about himself, the whole problem spilled out. "So now she's threatening to give up the flute if Mum stops her going to this party, which is crazy because she's so talented. She was on track to get accepted for a scholarship in Paris, but now I feel like she's about to throw it all away."

"It's probably just a phase; it's normal for kids her age to experiment."

"Yeah, but I'm worried she's out of her depth with this one. Avery's not… how do I put this?" His lips thinned for a moment. "She's not one of those kids who knows much about life and, erm, sex and stuff—bit of a late developer, I guess. She's never worried about what she looks like until recently, then suddenly she pulls out this dress and it's tiny and silver with sparkly things all over it, and, you know, kind of—" He gestured at an imaginary lowcut neckline. "And…" He stuck his leg out from under the table and made a slicing motion at the top of his thigh. "The hem's, like, right up *here…*"

He glanced up to see Judith frowning and folded his leg back under the table, feeling sheepish. "Sorry, am I sounding like a judgemental prick?"

"No, you sound like a concerned older brother."

"D'you reckon I made a mistake talking Mum into letting her go?"

"No, actually I don't. When Pippa was fourteen she took a whole lot of risks, staying out late, not letting our parents know where she was, that kind of stuff. Mum and Dad had no idea what to do with her. So, they grounded her. Took away her phone, picked her up and dropped her at school every day. They were really strict."

"Did it work?"

She shook her head. "No, it just made her more secretive. Unbeknown to any of us, Pip would climb down the tree next to her bedroom window at night. No-one could work out why she was so tired at school. Mum was convinced she had glandular fever. They took her to several doctors, but the tests were all negative. Then one night we got a call from the police to let us know she'd been caught spray painting hoardings with her gang. Luckily she was linked in with a school counsellor who was fantastic." Her voice warmed. "She helped Pippa to find other outlets. For Pip it was sport. She still loves netball, plays twice a week with her team. Her energy just needed to be directed into something that wouldn't stuff up her life. Now she's a qualified sports physio."

"Wow!" Carts threw himself back in his chair. "That's an amazing story."

"Yeah. Not that it happened overnight. Pippa pushed back—at Mum particularly. They've never really seen eye to eye." She frowned, and he wished he could reach out and smooth the little crease away from her forehead. "The thing is, if my parents had allowed her to experiment a bit more... not been so rigid with the rules, maybe she wouldn't have felt the need to rebel."

"I see what you mean."

"Perhaps Avery needs to try out new things to know what she really wants. I bet it will end up being her music."

"Maybe." He paused. "Do you mind if I ask you something, like, personal?"

She laid her knife and fork down neatly on her plate. "Of course, anything."

"Well—I mean at school, being quite, um, tall. As a girl. What was that like for you?"

She took a slow sip of her wine, and he worried he'd brought back memories she didn't want to talk about. "Avery is about your height, that's why I ask. She's terrified of growing any taller."

"I know how she feels." A little grimace. "To be honest, school wasn't great for me. I wasn't in with the cool crowd or sporty. It would probably have helped if I'd been like Pippa in that regard. But I was the quiet skinny *tall* girl who loved hanging out in the art room and barely spoke. Not a great recipe for popularity. How about you?"

Carts suppressed a grimace. "Horrible in my early teens. I had a massive growth spurt at thirteen and was mega skinny and nerdy. The perfect combo for being picked on. Then when I was fourteen, this super-cool, confident kid arrived at the school and for some reason took a shine to me. That's my mate, Aaron, who's in the UK, I think I may have mentioned him to you before." She nodded. "Having him in my corner meant I wasn't the weirdo they'd all labelled me as. Things got better after that. Can't say I ever had a lot of friends, but I did okay."

"He sounds nice—Aaron."

"Yeah, he's a great guy. Majorly conceited on the outside, especially about his hair, soft as a marshmallow on the inside. He'll be back in about six weeks... You'll meet him. Maybe." *No assumptions. No assumptions.* Nor was he going to tell her how they'd both fallen for Alice. He did, however, mention how Alice worked in her mum's shop, the Book Genie, because anyone who loved reading would know that ramshackle marvel of a second-hand book shop in Northbridge.

Sure enough, Judith clasped her hands in front of her face and said, "Oh, I love that place. And Alice... straight brown hair and glasses, right? She was really helpful when I was looking for a book one time. She's Polly's best friend." He nodded and she added, "Polly and I didn't really become friends until Alice left Perth. I think Polly decided I'd do as a back-up."

"Don't say that. You're the nicest friend anyone could wish for."

"I—oh." She shrugged. "I didn't try very hard to make friends when I was younger. I'm close to Pippa, and being with Mark, I suppose I didn't make a lot of effort." She gave a little huff and placed her napkin next to her finished meal. "And that was a big mistake. You get to your late twenties and when things blow apart, you're like... now what?"

He nodded. "I get that. Investing too much energy in love."

"Well, the wrong love, anyway." She shifted her chin onto her cupped hands. "Do you think you know?" The glow in her eyes sent his temperature soaring. "When you meet someone? Like, do you think you can fall in love at first sight?"

Was she trying to tell him something? Or was it simply wishful thinking? He flailed around, trying to form a sentence that was both witty and wise. And promptly opened his mouth and fucked it up. "I wouldn't have a clue. I'm the world's biggest failure in the love stakes."

And whoosh, just like that, the energy changed.

You could almost hear the music grinding to a slow and discordant halt. The guitar strings twanging as they snapped. A total A-grade disaster. The only way out of this was a subject change. He motioned desperately for the waiter. "I think we should look at the dessert menu, don't you?"

For the rest of the meal he laughed, he talked—too much and too fast —and it felt like Judith was slipping away from him with every stupid word that came out of his mouth.

Misery settled heavy in his gut as she politely refused dessert. Instead, they shared a trendy pot of bitter-tasting green tea while he yabbered on about how the soundproofed panels in the restaurant made it easier to hear each other's conversation. Only, what the fuck was the point of that when nothing you said was worth hearing?

As they stood outside the restaurant, he stared at the pavement and waited for the axe to fall.

Then Judith said, "Would you like to get a gelato?"

Carts' head spiked up, a grin spreading across his face. "Gelato! That sounds like a plan."

Judith smiled back, her eyes sparkling, and suddenly everything was right in the world.

"There's the best place down on the quay." She touched his arm; brief, yes, but enough to make his skin goosebump with anticipation. "Their gelatis are to die for."

"Cool." Inside Carts' head, Spandau Ballet pitched in with the opening lines of "Gold".

The gods of love had given him a reprieve.

Yep. Pure gold.

CHAPTER 5

"The white chocolate cherry delight is my favourite," Judith heard herself chirp. Normally her mouth would be watering at the mere mention, but she wasn't the slightest bit interested in the gelati. She wasn't ready to say goodbye and if she didn't do something, she had a hunch Carts was going to stare at his feet and let her drift away.

She knew the exact moment it happened. She'd got a bit too intense and scared him with her how-do-you-know-if-it's-love question. The kiss last weekend had raised her expectations and—unusual for her—she'd let her heart get in the way of common sense.

So, as they'd both stood awkwardly outside the restaurant, she shoved her sensible occupational therapist hat firmly back on her head and tried to work out what she'd do if she was helping a patient plan a social outing.

She'd tell them to drop the expectations.

She'd tell them to go eat gelati, have fun.

And by the look on Carts' face when she suggested it, either he *did* want to spend more time with her, or he was mad on gelati.

She sighed with relief when he grinned and said, "Sounds like a plan."

"Have you seen the kiosk on the quay?" she asked. "It's shaped like a diamond."

"Oh," a look of comprehension dawned, "is that's what that thing is? Always wondered."

"How could you not know it sold gelati?"

"You're right. Very unobservant." They fell into easy step now and it was so nice not to have to narrow her stride.

"I usually come to the quay and grab something to eat at lunch time," Carts explained. "Then I walk over the bridge and watch the action on the river, so I never get as far as the kiosk. Besides, I don't eat ice-cream much, you know, keeping healthy these days..." He gave his very flat stomach a pat.

Doubt encroached. "We don't have to... if you'd prefer..."

He glanced down at her. *Down.* Oh, what a fantastic feeling!

"You want the truth?"

She peeked up at him from under her lashes. "Mmmm?"

"I'd eat glass shards if it meant spending more time with you."

Delight rendered her speechless and, not knowing what else to do, she flipped her bag at his arm. "I'd never want you to do that. Just buy me a gelato."

"Small price to pay." And now she sensed they were both grinning in the dark.

At the kiosk, Carts deliberated for ages on flavours, a fact that Judith could tell was driving the assistant to a needle point of frustration as the girl shoved the fourth taster at him.

"Maybe I'll settle for French vanilla." He cast her the same panicked look as when he'd been confronted with the wine menu earlier.

"The salted caramel is wonderful," she murmured close to his ear. The smell of sandalwood cologne on warm male met her nostrils.

"Done!" He dragged out his wallet. "One salted caramel and one white chocolate cherry delight in a—?" When he glanced at her she could see there were actual caramel glints in his dark eyes.

"I'll take a cup," she answered weakly, feeling her body's response in her tightening nipples.

"Righto. Both in cups," Carts said gruffly to the assistant. A little muscle ticked in his jaw. She had the sudden urge to reach up and run her fingers around the short stubble and down his neck to where his unbuttoned shirt showed a glimpse of skin.

When he handed her the cup, she grasped it hard.

As they sat down on a bench overlooking the river, they both stretched their legs out.

Carts dug his spoon into his gelato. She twirled hers around and around and watched the cherry pieces glisten in the lights of the quay.

Carts let out a big sigh. "Don't you love evenings like this?"

"So much. You can still see the glow from the sun, and it must have set an hour ago."

"There's really nowhere better," Carts added.

"Have you ever wanted to live somewhere else?"

He put a spoonful in his mouth. "Yum," he said, pointing at the little tub. "You were right, this is *really* good. I thought about getting a job in Melbourne, but you know, leaving family and friends didn't appeal that much, and in the end, evidently, I stayed put. Not exactly Bear Grylls am I."

"You just know what you want."

He shrugged. "Maybe. And you?"

"Same. Looks like neither of us will make it onto the next series of *Survivor*."

"Darn it. I was going to take you bungee jumping next time. Urm— if there is a next time?"

She gave him a playful nudge, felt him return the pressure and even that was enough to make her pulse hop and skip. "Only if you promise no bungee jumping."

"Promise."

A moment's silence followed while they studiously spooned gelati into their mouths.

"I love boats," Carts said, waving his spoon towards the expanse of water. "That's why I come here really, to look at the boats."

"Do you sail?"

"Nah, I did rowing at school for a while, but then I got back pain so I stopped and never caught up. Oh, and restless legs syndrome, which was all part and parcel of my crazy growth spurt. I still fidget, though I have to say yoga's helped with that."

He drew his legs in.

"There's nothing to stop you learning now."

"I guess you're right. It's weird how you tell yourself it's too late to start new things."

"It's never too late," she said, her heart aching at how this gorgeous guy had clearly limited himself with his beliefs. "I had a patient recently who'd always wanted to play chess, but spent his life telling himself he didn't have the brain for it. We found him a local chess group. He's eighty-four and sharp as a tack and he came in after winning his first game with the biggest smile on his face."

"That gives me hope I guess—at thirty." He looked up from under ruffled brows, and as his lips quirked, little crinkles shunted around his eyes. "You're so encouraging to be around."

"Am I?"

"Yes, when I'm with you it feels like anything's possible, you've got this energy, like you believe in me—in people, I mean generally, not just me." He dug fast into his gelato and shovelled it into his mouth. It made her want to take the spoon and the cup and ditch them in the nearest bin then wrap her arms around him and...

"I do believe in people," she said breathlessly. "You, especially."

He gave a nervous laugh. Out the corner of her eye she saw his knee start to jiggle.

"Shall we walk?" he asked abruptly. Had she said something wrong? She'd never been this open about her feelings on a first date. Though, come to think of it, she'd never really had a first date as such.

"Okay," she said and jumped up.

"Finished?" Carts held his hand out for her cup. She placed it in his and watched as he strode purposefully towards the bin. When he'd tossed them in, he came back and said, "I always notice where the bins are. I hate people who leave rubbish around. It's so inconsiderate."

She beamed. She'd spent her time clearing up after Mark, ditching his sweet wrappers, telling him to put things in recycling. It was a little thing, but maybe it was the little things that showed you that you were compatible. Putting the toilet seat down, the cap back on the toothpaste. "I agree," she said, and as they headed off, she realised their feet were in perfectly synchronised steps. Their hands touched briefly as their arms swung and she thought how lovely it would be to link her fingers with his and stroll through the balmy evening hand in hand.

Would she dare? Take his hand first?

"Why don't we walk over the bridge, and you tell me something about the boats," she suggested.

He flicked her a surprised look. "You honestly want to know?"

"I honestly do."

By now they'd walked across the footbridge, commenting on how pretty the lights around Elizabeth Quay were as they changed from blue to green to pink to mauve. They'd stopped a couple of times, turned back towards the city and he'd pointed out the building he worked in.

On the far side, they stood gazing across the expanse of water to the twinkling lights of south Perth.

Carts cast her a covert sideways glance.

Tendrils of hair had strayed across her cheek, courtesy of the evening breeze. She pushed them back from her face and put her hands on the railing. Tentatively, he placed his left hand next to hers.

Their pinkies touched. Sensation prickled up and down his spine, and then, because he was always on the alert for rejection, he panicked.

"See those red and green lights out there?" He lifted the hand that had been nudging hers and pointed to the middle of the river. "They're called port and starboard markers."

Her skirt rustled. Had she moved away? *Damn!*

"What are they for?" she asked.

"They're for night-time navigation," he croaked. "Boats go through the markers so they don't hit a rock or a sand bank or something." Meanwhile, his heart had capsized and was sinking into the briny depths. He'd given completely the wrong signal. Go away. Not come closer. How in shite's name was he going to put this right?

"Oh, I see," Judith said. He was almost certain she'd edged closer.

Put your hand back on the rail, you moron.

With superhuman effort he reeled in his arm. Phew, now his hand was next to hers. He willed his muscles to relax. "Yeah, in a boat you always pass to the right of a starboard light and to the left of a port light, kind of, but it's a bit more complicated than that depending on whether you're going upstream or downstream."

By now he'd got his pinky to creep another agonising millimetre, and almost jumped as the edges of their hands came into contact. Neither of them moved.

"Like road rules but on water," Judith observed.

"Yeah."

It was now or never. Barely able to breathe, he lifted his hand and rested it gently over hers.

She shifted, as though about to tug her hand away.

Horror swamped him, an apology arcing up his throat, when suddenly her fingers curled around his. And squeezed.

Carts stared straight ahead until his eyes smarted. *Holy freakin' smoke.* They were… they were *actually* holding hands.

Runnels of delight sped up his arm, down his spine and sent alarming cues south of his waist. Luckily his new jacket would hide the evidence. Except he'd look like a complete dork trying to tug his jacket round his groin and hold her hand at the same time. And then what? Like, they were *only* at the hand-holding stage. What would happen if they freakin' kissed…?

Think of a blank screen.

He opened his mouth, tried to speak, but the trouble with blank screens was they cut off your access to words.

Luckily Judith asked, "So the green light is port?"

Somehow, he got his addled brain to form words. "Other way round. Green is starboard and red is port."

Was his hand getting sweaty? Would that put her off?

"You know a lot about boating for someone who's never sailed," Judith said.

"My dad used to own a yacht when I was a kid, nothing swanky or anything, just a dinghy really with one sail and an outboard motor. Most Sundays in summer Mum would pack a picnic lunch, and we'd go out on the river, do a bit of fishing and crabbing and stuff." Recalling those happier times loosened some of the tension in his muscles. And suddenly the reality of standing here holding Judith's hand sank in like golden syrup on pancakes.

"What a great way to spend your childhood," she mused. "My dad was always too busy with his building company to do things like that at weekends. Our idea of fun as kids was being taken to the newest display home. I remember one time Pippa scribbled all over the lounge room walls. I took the blame to stop her getting into trouble."

"Seriously, that's your most fun memory?"

"Probably not. It's just a vivid one. Pip was only three. Dad didn't believe me of course. I got told off for telling porky pies in front of a whole lot of home viewers." She sighed. "I do have a tendency to rescue people."

He glanced down at their joined hands, his big and bony knuckled, hers smooth-skinned and delicate, and fought the urge to shout, *don't rescue me. Don't hold my hand because you feel sorry for me.* Maybe Judith felt the energy in him shift because she glanced up. "It's really lovely, being here with you."

A frown of disbelief tugged at his eyebrows. "You're not just saying that?"

Her lashes swept down in a blink. "Sorry?"

"This, urm, holding my hand. The kiss. The other night. It's not about..." He stalled. Yep, his palms were definitely sweaty now.

She turned to face him. "About?"

"Being nice," he spluttered. "Like, you're a really kind person and I thought, maybe, you—"

"Why would you think that?" Her grip on his hand tightened and he clung on like a man drowning.

"No reason. I tend to say dumb things when I'm nervous," he finished with downcast eyes.

Which was why he didn't immediately notice Judith stepping closer until her hands were sneaking up his arms.

"Maybe we should kiss again," she murmured. "To prove I'm not just being nice."

CHAPTER 6

*J*udith sighed as his lips met hers. Their first kiss a week ago had been amazing. But this second one was even more heavenly, like falling into a bed of the sweetest, softest rose petals.

She let her arms creep around his waist, burrow under his jacket. He groaned against her mouth and his lips parted.

Vaguely she registered voices of people walking past, and realised they were right under the streetlamp. And because kissing in public places was new territory, she pulled back.

He blinked at her, his gaze hazy. "Wow!" was all he said, but it was enough, in this moment, for Judith Mellors, all of twenty-nine years old, to realise how truly magical a kiss between two people could be.

She was about to throw caution to the wind and dive in for another when a group of kids walked past, laughing. Carts stiffened.

"There's a quiet little spot just over here," she whispered, weaving her fingers into his. "Perhaps we should go there."

He nodded, so she led him down a winding path to her secret place. She often came and sat here at weekends, watching the water lap on the sandy river beach below, hidden from passers-by by a screen of grevilleas and eucalypts.

When she snuggled back into his chest he murmured against her ear, "Are you cold?"

"No, not cold. Just… kind of happy."

Carts rested his chin gently on the crown of her head. "Me too." A super-charged silence followed, his chest moving with his breath against hers, then he asked, "So you come here—like, on your own?"

"Mostly. Sometimes with Pippa."

"Not with your ex?"

"No, not with Mark. He never liked walking much. Or being in nature. He's heavily into computer games."

"Oh right." A pause. "If you don't mind me asking. Is it…" She sensed his feet shift. "Is it, like *properly* over between you two?"

"Oh yes. Absolutely over." She silenced the urge to tell him about Mark stealing her savings. That would mean more talking, and right now the mood was sensual and languorous, so why spoil something so special?

"You were with him a long time?"

"Twelve years."

"Wow, that's like loooong."

"And you? With—" She knew the girl was called Lucy. Polly had mentioned it.

"Lucy?"

"Yeah… Lucy…" Her voice trailed off. Did she really want to know? About Carts loving another woman? Kissing another woman? A churning feeling settled where her ribs met her stomach. She'd never deemed herself capable of jealousy, but was she? Was this a sign she was in deep? Already? She cleared her throat. "Were you two serious?"

"Kind of. We were together a year. That's long term for me."

Her gut constricted. What if Carts was one of those commitment-phobic men who came on all hot and strong and then lost interest? Wined and dined you and then *whoosh*. Gone. A couple of girls she knew had been… what did they call it? Ghosted or something. She'd been horrified when she heard, and retreated to her sewing room and washing Mark's socks, grateful that she wasn't out in the world getting ghosted.

"Perhaps we shouldn't talk about exes," she said. "Let's just enjoy tonight."

He murmured his agreement and they cuddled once more. To hell with worrying. She was far too practiced at that. Here now, in the present, she wanted to be daring, to take risks. So, when his arms tightened around her, she pressed her body along the length of his, delighting in how lean and muscular he was. She found where his shirt met his pants, gave it a little tug, and let her hands roam across the velvety skin of his stomach. The muscles of his abs quivered and he buried his face with a sigh into her hair.

"You smell divine," he murmured.

"So do you." She pressed her lips softly to his neck, saw his Adam's apple bob, once, twice, as if he was swallowing hard. She nipped little kisses lower, around his collar as her hands sneaked up his back.

"Oh Christ!" Deep and guttural, it was her cue to keep exploring. Her hands moved over his hips, around his butt, and then, daringly, she pulled him against her belly. The ridge of his erection strained against her, and a thought struck her that was utterly and completely out of character

Oh my, big boy!

Stifling a bubble of laughter, she lifted her lips and kissed him with a ferocity the Judith of yesterday would not have believed herself capable of.

MAN, OH, FREAKIN' *man!!!*

If he'd thought hand-holding had been a turn-on, think again.

The pressure of her lips, the wild tangle of their tongues… her hands roaming up his back, over his hips and pressing into his butt cheeks… and things were hotting up down below faster than a six-burner barbecue.

He tried to back off on the kiss, just for a moment, to regroup and claw back a skerrick of self-control…

But then with a little moan, Judith did some wicked rotational thing with her hips. And suddenly his cock was galloping full tilt for the finish line.

Holy fuck NO!—No way... not *here*...

Desperately he wrenched his lips from hers. Stumbled backwards.

She stared at him with a mix of puzzlement and hurt. He'd never want to hurt her, but neither did he want... Oh, Christ almighty, it had almost got very messy.

Wrapping his jacket around himself, he shook his head. "Shit, sorry, I —it's just—"

His cheeks were on fire. Miserable humiliation slugged him and all he wanted was to crawl under the nearest shrub and hide from her gaze.

He wasn't a real man. Real men had control over their libido. They didn't almost blow on a kiss.

She stepped back. He tried to grab her hand and missed.

"Did I do something wrong?" she asked

"No, it's not you," he said desperately, "it's me, I'm—" He tried to find words that wouldn't give the whole miserable game away. "Could we just, you know, take it slow? Get to know each other a bit better, first."

Judith's spine snapped straight. "Absolutely. Of course." Her voice was thin and strained and polite, as if she was talking to a stranger. With a flick of her hair, she turned and started walking. He followed, tried again to grab her hand but she was swinging her bag by the strap, and it banged into his leg. He stifled a yelp. What the frig did women put in their handbags to make them hurt that much when they bumped you?

"I didn't explain myself very well," he muttered miserably.

She stopped on the path and said, "It's okay Carts." She sighed. "Look, to be honest, this is a bit silly, isn't it? I mean, I'm only four weeks out of a long-term relationship, and I'm trying to seduce you behind a tree. I obviously misread the signs. I'm totally rusty about all this dating business to be honest." Her laugh was as paper thin as her voice. "Just forget I did that. Please."

"I loved it... honestly." He reached out and this time located her hand and lifted it, with the bag still attached. They both stared at it, and he felt her tug of resistance and quickly released it. Hand and bag dropped like a weight. Like the weight around his heart.

Judith looped the bag over her shoulder. "How about we meet at yoga next Friday, have a drink afterwards, just get back to where we were before."

His shoulders sagged and she must have noticed because she said, "Hey, it's okay. Really. I'm not upset." Her tone was soothing as she rubbed his arm. He felt like one of her patients, and realised how good she was at making people feel better.

"I like you. I really do," he pleaded.

"Thank you. I like you too." She said so airily it almost disappeared before it reached his ears.

She started walking and silently he fell into step beside her.

In the darkness his mouth moved as he searched for words. *I very nearly came when you kissed me; my brain seems to have lost control of my dick...* variations came and went... No freakin' way could he say any of them.

So, he said nothing at all.

It was Judith who finally said, "I really should be getting home."

His heart bleeding with the realisation that he'd blown probably the most important date of his life, Carts replied politely, "Of course, I'll walk you back to your car."

CHAPTER 7

*W*hen Judith finally located Polly on Monday morning, she was typing up a report in the Echidna Ward staff office, her dark curls tugged into a tight knot on top of her head and her pretty mouth pulled into a grim line.

This was so unlike the usually ebullient Polly that Judith hesitated. "Is everything okay?"

"Yes of course."

"It's just you scooted off after the team meeting and you've kind of been…" Judith searched for words, feeling for some reason like she had to walk on eggshells.

Polly tapped her lips with her pen and lifted an eyebrow. "Been what?"

"A bit off," Judith supplied lamely, then gathered her courage. "Since Carts' birthday party, actually."

Polly gave a shrug. "Just busy." Then, narrowing her eyes, she went in for the kill. "But more importantly, how have *you* been since Carts' party?" Judith felt her skin tingle with a blush as Polly pushed on. "Have you met up again?"

Judith had confided in Polly after Carts' party about The Kiss (it always had capital letters in her head), so she guessed she only had herself to blame for Polly probing. She also knew that there was something Polly wasn't admitting to, or rather *someone*, in the form of the handsome locum psychiatrist, Dr Solo Jakoby, but she was too completely overwhelmed with her own problems right now to focus on it. Sinking down in a chair opposite Polly, she sighed. "To be honest, I'm confused."

Polly sat back, her face brightening. "Tell all. I need a distraction from writing this family therapy report." As well as being a social worker, and renowned for her counselling skills, in her personal life, Polly was a matchmaker extraordinaire. She had an amazing knack for getting people to talk about the most intimate details of their lives.

Like now.

Judith stared at her hands. "I think I've scared him off." She glanced up and, sure enough, Polly's interest was piqued.

"Not possible. I saw how he hung around you at his party, he couldn't even greet his other guests. Believe me, he's got it bad. But I do need the deets if you want my advice."

Judith squeezed her hands together. She really did need to offload; it had been going round and round in her head all weekend. "Okay, so we went out Friday on a date, and it was lovely. He took me to Blazers on Elizabeth Quay and insisted on paying, which I know is really old school, but it was nice because Mark never paid for anything, I even paid for my own birthday dinner last year." She took a deep breath. "Anyway, afterwards we had gelati and we talked and walked, and then he—you know, we, um, cuddled and *stuff* and I kind of got a bit enthusiastic."

"Go, you!"

Judith cringed. "No, no you don't understand—it all went horribly wrong."

"What did you do? Rip his pants off in public?"

"No, of course not. It's just I remembered what you said a couple of weeks back, about how women need to call the shots more often. I wanted to show him I was all in. But I think I took things too far."

"Uh-huh." Polly sounded thoughtful. "In what way?"

Judith felt the colour suffusing her cheeks. "In the kissing department." Her lips twisted into a rueful smile. "I even surprised myself."

Polly lifted one foot onto the edge of the desk and rocked her chair back. "Carts hasn't had a date for a year. You probably blew his fuses."

"He did say that."

"That you blew his fuses?"

"No, that he hasn't dated for a while."

"Oh dear. The poor guy's a sperm bank waiting to happen."

Judith's eyes widened. "Polly!"

Polly threw back her head with a wicked gurgle. "I swear you are easier to shock than Alice. I think that's why I love you, you two are so alike. Except she's got two left thumbs when it comes to craft. She can't even wrap a gift without sticking her fingers up with tape."

Judith grinned. It was nice to be compared to Alice. It made her feel like she might have finally made it into Polly's close-knit circle of friends.

"Anyway, I digress. What happened next?"

Judith sandwiched her cheeks with her palms. "Oh god, it's *so* embarrassing. Basically, he jumped away like I'd bitten him and said could we take it slow. Get to know each other first."

"And what did you say to that?"

"I agreed." Judith nodded emphatically to make her point. "In fact, I said to him, that *obviously* I—I shouldn't be getting involved with anyone this quickly after Mark."

Polly looked baffled. "Why not?"

"How could I take Carts back to my place...? There's still a bottle of Mark's shampoo in the shower, and some of his work clothes in the wardrobe. It wouldn't be nice."

"Oh, fuck a doodle, is that all?" Polly waved an airy hand. "Forget nice. Nice gets you nowhere. Alice was *nice* to Aaron, and he repaid her by sleeping off his hangovers on her couch and getting her advice on how to escape his latest dating disaster."

"But he fell in love with her? In the end," Judith said eagerly. She'd heard part of the story from Polly before. "Something must have changed?"

"She seduced him." Polly smirked and tapped a finger on her chest. "With a little advice from yours truly. He'd been in love with her all along, but men's brains don't always connect to their hearts. Something to do with their dicks interfering with the wiring."

Judith laughed; her mood already lifted. Polly had a knack of making you take things, even tragedies like Friday night, more lightly.

Polly leaned her elbows on the desk conspiratorially. "So what's your next move?"

"I think taking it slow is very sensible," she lied, trying not to let her mind revisit the purple-hued fantasies she'd been having all weekend.

Polly cast her a disbelieving look and Judith opened her mouth to solidify her stance when the door opened, and Solo's head popped around it.

"Ah, Judith, here you are. I've been looking everywhere for you. I need you to come and talk to a patient about anxiety management strategies."

Judith glanced at Polly. Her face had gone blank as her eyes snapped back to the computer screen. The room felt like someone had blasted it with icy air.

Solo ignored Polly. Polly ignored Solo.

Awkward. Very, very awkward.

Her gaze pinned to the screen, Polly said flatly, "Doctor's orders must be obeyed."

Judith thought Solo gave a snort.

What was wrong with these two?

But there was no point questioning it because the frostiness was turning into a blanket of icy tundra that was quite unpleasant to be around.

Solo lifted an eyebrow. "Was I interrupting something?"

Judith jumped to her feet. "No, nothing important," she said and followed him.

∼

CARTS DROVE to work listening to the Ramones on full volume to try and keep all thoughts of Judith out of his head. Which failed miserably when "Baby I Love You" blasted at full volume through the speakers.

He stabbed it off with a snarl.

The problem was the whole disastrous evening had been on replay inside his head all weekend. And none of his favourite music from the eighties seemed to alleviate the situation.

After his hard-on hash-up, they'd made stilted conversation until they reached Judith's car. She'd been searching for her keys in her bag, head bent when he'd decided to give her a quick kiss on the cheek. He'd missed and hit his chin hard on the crown of her head. She'd rubbed at the spot, and he'd reached out and rubbed it too, rather like he used to do to Avery when she'd bumped her noggin as a kid. Which might be the right thing for an older brother to do... but with the woman you were so hot for you could barely get the words out, let alone your dick to behave, it was wrong—as—fuck.

Sure enough, she'd given him a tight, polite smile before pecking *him* on the cheek in what could only be described as a *sisterly* way.

Doomed, utterly doomed.

After moping around the house all of Saturday, ending up half-cut at the Shamrock with Dan and Carts' new housemate Solo, who incidentally had been in a mighty foul mood this past week, he'd finally plucked up the courage as he zigzagged a path home at midnight to thumb into his cracked phone, *Thanks for a lovely evening yesterday. Hope to see you at yoga.*

He hadn't got a message back until halfway through Sunday morning. He swore his fucking stupid screen had got even more cracked, because reading it had been a challenge, but he'd managed to decipher, *Thank you, I really enjoyed it. See you at yoga. x*

His mood had leapt at the words "really" and "enjoyed". Then sank as he decided that *x* was definitely lukewarm. *xxx* would have been okay. An emoji of a heart would have been fantastic. Actually, amend that; *x* was probably cool, verging on cold. He guessed it was not as cold as her not replying at all, not in the super cold territory like when you were searching for the hidden pressie as a kid and your parents kept shouting cold, colder, *freezing.*

Not freezing. Which meant there was still a glimmer of hope.

On Sunday morning he'd tried to call Aaron in England, then realised it was the middle of the night in Cambridge. He thought about Aaron tucked up in bed next to Alice and the envy he'd thought all gone hit his gut, hard and sour. Yet again he'd found himself in a game he didn't understand the rules to, flailing around trying to work out what the hell to do next. Looking in from the outside, like some ragged, grimy-faced kid in a Dickens novel.

By Sunday afternoon his grumpiness had reached new heights. A fat lot of use his year off women had been. He should never have taken Polly's advice on that. He was now so out of practice he'd almost made an abject fool of himself.

Finally, desperate for a solution, he'd sat down at his laptop and googled premature ejaculation. Because while he knew he hadn't exactly been Casanova before, he'd never been at risk of *this.* Her kiss, her touch, the way she'd pulled him close and pressed her beautiful body into him, had fundamentally done him in.

And then he'd blown it, by intimating he wanted to take it slow. He hadn't meant the relationship part, and, no, of course he hadn't meant *not* kissing each other. Jeesh, Judith's kisses were the best. It was like their lips had been designed by some divine being to fit together perfectly. A kissing prototype made in heaven.

But… but… what if he couldn't *perform?*

He guessed pulling back was better than the other possibility… though crickets, it had been a close call.

His eyes scanned the google list of treatments for ejaculatory problems. Finally, he clicked on one from a health channel that looked viable and wasn't trying to sell him snake oil.

Okay, anxiety could cause it. Yes, tick that box. He was terrified. What was he supposed to do about that? He read on.

Avoid sexual encounters and focus on other aspects of the relationship. Well, hmm, that was all very well, but Judith clearly was hot for him, a fact that still filled him with disbelief. How long could he keep rejecting her advances? Hell, he was equally hot for her. He just needed to manage the major glitch in his anatomy.

Okay, what next?

The pause, squeeze technique. Carts' eyes widened in horror. This one involved getting close to your orgasm, then asking your partner to squeeze the base of your penis. Oh, *Jesusssss.* He got up and paced the room, raking fingers through his hair. This was not his idea of making love for the first time with Judith. Gazing deeply into her eyes and asking, *would you mind giving my dick a squeeze...? No, not there, a bit lower down...*

He forced himself to sit back at his computer and scrolled down the screen. *Reduce sensitivity by wearing a condom.* Fair enough, that was one piece of sound advice. He'd always been super considerate with safe-sex practices because of course it was as much the guy's responsibility as the woman's. But then, what if she wanted to roll the condom on him and he came while she was—he groaned out loud. Oh, fuck NO!

He tried to calm his erratic breathing. Went over to his record collection and studied the spines. Playing some of his favourites from the eighties was usually guaranteed to improve his mood. He removed the first cover that came to hand and his eyes fell on "Tainted Love". That got shoved back quickly. Next came Marvin Gay's "Sexual Healing". Freakin' unbelievable. Okay, he'd pull one out at random and not look at the title. He dusted the vinyl, placed it carefully on the turntable and put the needle to it. Out came the opening bars of Frankie Goes to Hollywood's "Relax, (don't do it)". He managed a twisted grin at that; there was clearly no escaping his problems through music. He went back to his laptop, chewing hard on the inside of his lip, and read the next gem of wisdom.

Masturbate before a date. Not bloody likely. He got so nervous before seeing Judith his libido sank to below zero and he was worried nothing at all would happen, and then—*whoosh,* it was heading for the line like the favourite on Melbourne Cup Day. He groaned. Besides, if he did manage to masturbate you could guarantee with his luck, it would end up like that scene out of *There's Something About Mary* and he'd smear gism in Judith's beautiful hair.

Totally distracted by thoughts of his weekend misery, Carts found he'd arrived at work without remembering a single traffic light or stop sign. He reached for his entry card and swiped it and a minute later swerved into Ron's parking spot, relishing the squeal of his tyres on the concrete. Hopefully he'd left rubber marks. Still, it was good not to have to take the train in to work this week. He had to be grateful for the small things right now, because the big ones were at risk of submerging him.

As he gathered up his briefcase and KeepCup, his phone rang.

Aaron. At last. He grabbed it and almost shouted a relieved, "Mate!"

"Maaate. How are you?"

"All the better for hearing from you. Hey, isn't it late over there?"

"Yeah, nearly midnight. But I saw you called yesterday," Aaron hesitated, "and I've been meaning to phone you anyway."

"How's things going in the green and pleasant land?"

"Good. Alice has been trying to educate me about culture and not doing a bad job, to be honest. We spent yesterday on the museum strip in London. Like seriously, the English love preserving old shit, but I have to say, I'm almost getting the appeal."

Carts laughed. "So you'll be sending home a container of eighteenth-century chamber pots."

"Not quite. Though Alice has found a few antiques. And of course, Rowena's bought up big on leather-bound first editions for the Book Genie. Anyway, how are you, mate?"

"Much the same as when you left." Aaron and Alice had gone to visit her father in Cambridge, closely followed by Rowena, Alice's mum. They'd only been gone three months, but at times like this, when he really needed his best mate, it felt more like three years.

Carts changed ears as he opened the car door. "I've been hanging out with Dan a bit. Work's been bloody awful, but I'm in charge this week, because the old bastard's gone on leave."

"That must be a relief." Aaron knew his long-term problem with Ron, they'd stuck pins in him, metaphorically speaking, enough times over a few pints.

"Still doing yoga?"

"You bet."

"Got up to a thousand sun salutes yet?"

"Two thousand, mate. Every morning without fail. I'm a demi-god."

"Always knew it." Aaron laughed. A pause. "Seeing anyone?"

Carts kicked the car door wide with his foot. "Kind of. I guess. There's this girl... a friend of Polly's actually. We'll see where it goes."

"Awesome. Polly does have great taste in friends."

Carts grinned despite himself. "Sure does." He muffled a sigh. "We're taking it slowly, both of us have been a bit burnt. How are you and Alice?"

Another pause. "Now you've asked... Has Polly said something, by any chance?"

"Nope. Barely seen Polly lately. She's gone a bit weird."

"Tell me something I don't know." Aaron and Polly had always clashed. Something to do with them both being big personalities.

"Anyway," Aaron took a deep breath on the end of the line, "I do have some news. I've been kind of putting off telling you because... well, you know..."

"Jeesh man, get to the point."

"Alice and I have got engaged."

Carts' throat constricted. "Wow! Happy for you both, mate," he gulped out. "Been expecting it, to be honest." He had. And yeah, bloody oath he was happy for them, absolutely over the moon, but the truth was, the timing was bad. If his Friday evening had gone better, he'd be boogying in the parking lot. He hated the stab of envy that got in the way of feeling fantastic at his best mate's happiness. This was the guy who'd stood by him through thick and thin, who'd always been there to pat him on the back and buy him a beer after his latest romance went down the gurgler. He swallowed the bitter taste. "Hope I'm still the best man?"

"You bet."

"Forgot to ask, did she say yes?"

Aaron laughed. "Yeah, well I probably don't deserve it, but she did, and I feel like the luckiest bastard in the world right now."

"Best news, mate. Congratulations to you both. When's the wedding?"

"No plans yet. Oliver's is next spring, so we'll get through that first. With Naomi being a wedding planner you can bet that's going to be the Aussie equivalent of the Hollywood wedding of the year."

"That fits." Carts was in awe of Aaron's older brother Oliver, a finance guru to the young and hip, super good-looking, but also a bloody nice guy. His popular books on managing your finances took pride of place on Carts' bookshelf. He'd not met Naomi, but there was a picture of the two of them together on the back cover of Oliver's latest book. All smiles, perfect teeth, perfect hair, her hand on Oliver's knee with a sparkling diamond on her finger.

There was no way the Blake brothers would ever need advice on managing premature ejaculation.

After a few more words about weddings, Aaron yawned on the end of the line. "Think I'll call it a night. I'll sleep easy now I know you're okay with it."

"Christ almighty, how could I not be?"

"Knowing you'd had a bit of a thing for Alice a while back, I guess I was worried. Didn't want to upset you."

"That's all water under the bridge. Don't get me wrong, Alice is wonderful, *gorgeous*… way too good for you, it's just…"

"You're taken with this girl, aren't you?"

He tried to sound airy. "Yeah, I am, sort of… It's just—"

"Sounds like there's a qualifier in there?"

Carts hesitated. Maybe if they were at the pub, after a couple of Guinnesses he'd have the courage to blurt out about his dick dysfunction. But it wasn't something you told your mate who was 20,000 kilometres away and inhabiting a different universe. One where love came easy.

"Nah, nothing. It's going fine. You know me, not high on the confidence stakes."

"Just relax mate. If she's the one, it will work out, like me and Alice. But hey, if you want to talk it through, give me a call sometime this week."

"I don't need to talk about it." *Yes, yes, I fucking do.* "It's going great, early days and all."

"Cool. What's her name?"

"Judith."

"Keep me posted on developments with Judith."

"Sure will. Catch you later."

"Call me, okay? Don't be a fucking stranger, mate."

"Will do."

Pressing the red icon, Carts grabbed his briefcase before exiting the car.

He had a day of back-to-back clients, most probably sorting out the things his boss should have done regarding their tax offsets and work entitlements.

He didn't have any qualms about that.

He was good at putting numbers into neat little boxes on spreadsheets and making sure they all added up.

If only relationships were that easy.

CHAPTER 8

$\mathcal{J}$udith parked her car outside Mark's apartment and peered up at the third-floor windows. He must be home, because Mark never went out after work. Somewhere in there he'd be gaming, his desk all set up with his space age-looking computer fit-out. The equipment she'd helped him pay for.

Resentment rose up her throat.

All weekend she'd kept trying to contact him. No return calls, not even a text message. So, this morning she'd gathered up a bag of his left-over bits and pieces and resolved that after work she'd front up and have it out with him.

She was anxious and jittery as she went up the steps and pressed the bell for apartment four.

No reply. She pressed again, longer this time.

She'd sent a text message just before leaving work. *Mark, I'm worried about you. I'm coming over NOW.*

Finally, after what seemed like an eternity, Mark's voice crackled over the intercom. "Yeah?"

"Mark, it's me, Smidge."

She winced. Without thinking, she'd used his old pet name for her. Maybe it was just relief that he wasn't dead.

"Oh, hi."

"Can I come up?"

"Er—okay. Give me a minute."

It crossed her mind that he might have a woman up there, which she immediately dismissed. Mark had let himself go these past couple of years as his gaming obsession increased. If she hadn't been such a loyal soul, she wondered, would she have stuck around?

She stood hugging her elbows, looking out across the expanse of rooftops to the ocean visible on the horizon. At least he had nice views, not that he'd even bother to raise his head and look out the window.

The door buzzed and she pushed it open and entered the foyer, then made her way swiftly up the three flights of stairs. The door to number four was slightly ajar.

The apartment smelt of takeaway fast food. She flicked a look in the bedroom, which was a seething mass of discarded clothing. She resisted clucking her tongue. The open-plan living area with its tiny kitchenette was at the end of the passage, she remembered, because she'd helped him bring some furniture and boxes in. Another door to the left was closed. She knew what was in there. Mark's huge black desk and leather chair surrounded by a cockpit of screens. Curtains closed to shut out anything but his gaming universe. It was the only thing he seemed to care about these days, because he'd long ago stopped caring about her.

A pang of sadness constricted her ribs. What a wasteland their relationship had ended up. Two young people who should still be enjoying life and each other, locked together in a habit that had made them both miserable.

And now it seemed she was clueless about how to get out there and date again. She pushed all thoughts of a certain brown-eyed guy out of her head; she had a job to do.

Mark was slouched on the sofa.

She took in the pallor of his skin, the dark shadows under his eyes and the fact his belly had got slacker even since they'd split up.

"Well at least you're alive," she said. He lifted a surprised eyebrow. "I was worried, Mark. You haven't responded to any of my messages."

"I've been busy."

"Too busy to call me back?"

"Sorry about that," he muttered.

She dumped the plastic bag on the coffee table. "I've brought some stuff you left behind."

"Right." He didn't look at her, just pointed the remote at the TV. A popular reality show appeared on the screen; women with big lips and boofy hair screeching at each other.

She went and perched on the easy chair next to the sofa. It was the one that used to be in her craft room. She'd had plans to re-cover it in a nice bright print, ready for when they finally bought a house together. But in the end, they'd had to split their furniture and she knew she wouldn't get around to doing anything with this one.

"There's your Grateful Dead T-shirt and a pair of your work overalls in there. I've bagged up your toiletries. Shampoo, and your shaving cream." She'd be glad to be rid of his anti-dandruff treatment. "Your exercise ball is in the boot of my car." She'd been trying to get him to do stretches, even practise some yoga with her. No luck.

"I don't need the ball."

"You *should* use it, Mark. All that sitting at the computer, it's not good for you. You know sitting's the new smoking, don't you?"

He rolled his eyes and flicked channels. David Attenborough, she thought abstractly, as a school of iridescent fish shimmied through a coral reef.

He sifted a hand through his sandy hair. "Will you stop banging on about my health? I'm fine."

She bit her lip. He was right. His health wasn't her responsibility; it never had been.

"Besides, I'm too busy to exercise right now."

"What with?"

"A project."

"Work?" she asked, incredulous. Mark worked in officially the most boring job in the world, as warehouse manager of a packaging company. She knew why he never went for a promotion. The job didn't take energy away from his gaming.

"Christ no, wouldn't waste my time on that shithole."

65

Her stomach tightened. She had to say what she'd come here for. She drew in a breath.

"Mark, there's another reason I'm here. I guess you know what it is."

He flicked channels back to the boofy-haired brigade. "Yeah?"

"Could you turn that down while we're talking, please?"

He flipped the TV to silent, but kept his eyes fixed on the screen.

Judith pinched her thigh, a habit she had when she went to the dentist and was waiting for them to put the needle in her gum. "When I went shopping on Friday, the sale wouldn't go through because there weren't enough funds in our—my—savings account." She waited, but Mark said nothing. "So, when I got home, I checked the balance, and the account has no money in it."

He cast her a sullen look and grunted.

"Deposits were withdrawn of nine hundred dollars on three consecutive days last week. They went into your new account."

Mark rolled his neck with some loud clicks. "I borrowed it. I'll pay it back in a couple of months. Three max."

Her stomach bottomed out. Even when she heard him say it, she couldn't quite believe that he'd taken her money so brazenly. "Why?"

"For a game me and the guys are developing."

"A game?"

"Yes Smidge, a game. We've been designing it for months."

"You've never mentioned it," she said, pulling a strand of hair over her shoulder and smoothing it with shaky fingers.

He tapped the side of his nose. "Top secret," he said, and gave her his cheesy, lazy-eyed look. The one she used to find kind of endearing, but which now made her stomach rise up her throat.

"Who are *we*?"

"VampEmperor and Trojanwarrior—oh yeah, and some input from Bashcityboy."

"Can't you use their real names?"

"We don't bother with them anymore. Our gaming identities are more the real us."

Wasn't that the truth.

She shook her head. "I don't get it—if you're just coming up with an idea, why on earth did you need the money?"

"To hire a graphic artist to draw up characters, do the world building... It must look professional before we present it. It's a competitive market out there, Smidge."

She shook her head. "I can't believe you just took it without asking."

"There wasn't time. I needed it—" he snapped his fingers, "like yesterday. I meant to tell you but I—um—forgot."

She heard herself laugh, almost hysterically. "Like you forgot to answer my calls this weekend." The now-familiar chin-wobble threatened. If she cried, he'd get exasperated and she'd feel like a pathetic fool.

"Sorry Smidge. It's just we're so frigging busy nutting out the final prototype. When we hear back—"

"Hear back from whom?" Bewilderment made her shake her head.

"The company in Silicon Valley. We're deep in discussions at the moment. C'mon, be nice, I just need a few more weeks."

The truth dawned. "Is this why you didn't want to come on holiday?"

"Kind of. But really, Smidge, the idea of hiking around Scotland wasn't exactly tugging my chain."

Looking at him, she had to agree. How blind had she been, thinking they could salvage their relationship with a walking holiday? But the fact he had been deceiving her, working on all of this behind her back, added an extra sting.

"And what if this project doesn't come off?" She schooled her voice not to shake. "What happens then?"

He stared at the TV screen absently. "I'll pay you back. In instalments or something."

She let out an exasperated huff. She knew all about Mark paying her back. The desk, the ridiculously expensive computer system. She needed to stop colluding with him.

Jumping up, she threw up her hands in a gesture she hoped showed how upset she was. He didn't even look at her. "Not in two or three months, Mark. A month, maximum. Promise me."

"Okay, promise." He smiled, heaved himself off the sofa and yanked up his pants. "You off then?" She heard the relief in his voice. He looked like he was going to give her a kiss, but she pulled back. The idea of him touching her was abhorrent.

"Don't be angry, Smidgy." Mark's lower lip jutted into a mock sulk. And she realised that's what he'd always done. Made out she was being unreasonable when all she'd ever wanted was for him to act like an adult.

She stalked towards the door. She'd promised herself on the way here she'd stand her ground. She turned around and forced herself to look at him, sprawled on the couch, with his gaze glued back to the giant screen. "I want it back. Every single cent, and no excuses."

As she took the stairs, she felt a flicker of something like pride in her belly.

She hadn't caved in.

It was a step in the right direction.

STREAMS OF KIDS in dark blue and grey uniforms flooded out the gates of St Catherine's College. One bumped Carts with his backpack and didn't even notice. Gangly arms hung at the boy's sides, shoulder blades visible even through his school shirt. Carts couldn't help a wry smile. It reminded him of how he used to be, bones sticking out every which way and not enough flesh to cover them. Surreptitiously he gave his stomach a pat and was reassured to hit a ridge of hard muscle. Yoga had been doing wonders for his abs, he realised. It had been gradual, but after a year he was building a not so bad bod.

He scanned the group of girls coming towards him, a sea of laughing faces, then he spotted Avery a good head taller than the purple ponytail bobbing along next to her. He guessed that had to be Zammy.

Avery's face was relaxed. He was good at reading her features; she looked happy, if a little too eager to please, like she was hanging off the other girl's every word.

When she spotted him, her smile broadened into a grin, and she waved.

As they got closer, he realised where Avery had got the weird kohl habit happening with her eyes. Zammy's were rimmed completely in black. She was wearing purple lipstick. Did they allow them to do that at school nowadays or had she put it on in the bathroom afterwards?

Then he caught himself. He sounded like a wrinkly old prune—another of the arsenal of insults Avery sometimes hurled at him.

He made sure he slouched against the wall, dug his hands deep in his pockets and tried for a cool grin in return.

"Hi trouble," he said

"Yo, bro." Avery lifted her hand in the air, palm facing him, which he realised he was meant to slap. He took his hand out of his pocket and held it up to her. A boy following her swivelled and looked at them as he passed. Suddenly Avery wrapped him in a bear hug. Why did he think this was for show? Not that she wouldn't hug him, but this was a "hey look at me" kind of hug.

Zammy observed them with a sulky turn to her lips, and something inside him flipped like a fish on a line. Like this girl was going to be trouble for his little sister in a way he couldn't quite put words to but knew in some deep recess of his being.

Avery tossed the hair off her forehead. "Zammy, this is my big bro, Carter."

"Yeah," said Zammy. She blew a bubble of gum, grape-coloured like her ponytail. It snapped and she reeled it back with her tongue and kept chewing, still watching him out of impassive eyes.

Carts shifted his feet. Christ, how could a sixteen-year-old be this intimidating?

"What you doing here?" Avery cocked her head at him.

"I thought I'd pick you up from school since I'm coming to dinner."

"It's not Wednesday."

"I know. But Dad's out tomorrow at some work function, so I told Mum I'd come Tuesday."

"Zammy and I are going to the mall. To choose make-up for her party."

"No worries. I can drop you and wait."

"You've got a car?" Zammy's eyes sparked sudden interest.

"Yep, sure do." Carts was proud of his immaculate Mazda 6. He washed and vacuumed it most weekends, and it had just been polished. Another job he'd done on Sunday to get his head away from ejaculatory issues and Judith.

"Cool," Zammy drawled. "It'll give us more shopping time if we don't have to walk. Can you give Boner a ride too?"

Carts blinked. "Who?"

"Boner." Zammy smirked between chews. "His surname's Bone. But he got the name for other reasons." Her eyes challenged him. As if he was going to take the bait on that one.

Finally, a big youth with an angry looking rash of spots along his jaw joined them, and then another smaller one with close-set eyes who muttered that his name was Lewis. They all muscled into the back of his car, except Avery, who got in the front seat and immediately preened herself in the passenger mirror.

Carts supposed things could be worse.

He could be called Boner.

Sometime later he was sitting in Blue Heaven café waiting... and waiting. Ghastly tuneless elevator music piped out of an invisible speaker above his head. An elderly couple sat drinking coffee out of paper cups and staring into space with stolid-looking pastries in front of them. Babies and children screamed and were hushed by exhausted-looking mothers. A machine whizzed and creamy milkshakes were poured and handed to a seething mass of uniformed kids.

It seemed like the whole of St Catherine's College congregated here after school.

Carts, sipping on a cappuccino, surveyed the group of teenagers moving as one. It was like they had an identity that was more than their individual selves, a group consciousness that made them somehow more powerful, like an army of locusts that descended on Summerside Mall every afternoon around three-thirty, stomping and munching everything in their wake.

Then he thought of Judith's words about Avery, that maybe her flute wasn't enough right now. He thought about his own longing to be accepted when he was much the same age as Avery. How the bullying had scarred him, not visibly, but at some deep level. Despite Aaron's friendship, he'd never quite recovered, had he? Sure, he'd learnt to armour himself, but there were places where the soft parts of his soul still hadn't healed. It showed in his failed relationships with women; in how he allowed Ron to keep abusing him at work.

It showed in his lack of adventurous spirit, his unwillingness to try new things.

Like learning to sail. It wasn't too late, Judith had said. Could he step out from his safe little cave of collecting eighties LPs, and his evenings at the Shamrock? Except... he had—with taking up yoga, hadn't he? He was proud of that. Damn proud, in fact.

He breathed in, muttered a couple of OMs under his breath, and wondered whether it would look too keen to message Judith. It was Tuesday, after all.

He picked up his phone and thumbed in, *I'm with my little sis at the mall. She's buying make-up with her friend. Talking it through with you helped.*

His fingers hovered over the send icon.

Then, letter by letter, he deleted it from his cracked screen. He couldn't risk any more pain right now.

When he glanced up his eyes snagged on Avery over near the drinks counter. She was leaning against a post with her skirt hitched up—he could tell, because her jumper had ridden up and you could see the bunched-up waist band. Carts' eyes narrowed at her long skinny legs with the socks wrinkled down around her clunky Doc Martens... he guessed that was the look girls went for these days.

But there was another look happening that he really didn't like. It was the one the boy with Avery was giving her. And the fact that he wasn't a boy as such. He had slicked-back blonde hair and a foxy face. What worried Carts more was, he wasn't wearing school uniform. Instead he was dressed in oil-stained jeans and a denim jacket. He was the type of guy a girl of sixteen might think was kind of cool, but by Carts' summation, he was at least eighteen or nineteen.

Carts frowned as Avery's hand came out and gave the guy's arm a playful punch. He leered—yes, that was definitely a leer—then leaned forward and whispered something in Avery's ear. She wiggled her shoulder into him with a giggle then pulled back, batting her eyelashes.

Foxy face gave her another lascivious grin, and Avery tossed her head and sashayed back to Zammy in the milkshake queue. Even from here Carts could tell she was blushing.

The interlude made unease jackknife in his gut.

That guy was no school kid.

And frankly, his intentions did not look honourable.

Not. At. All.

When he finally rounded up his band of four and got them back to the car, Carts couldn't stop the troubling thoughts about foxy face in the denim jacket. By the time he'd dropped off the rest of the gaggle at their respective homes around the suburb, it burst out of his mouth. "Who was that bloke?"

"What bloke?"

"That one you were talking to in the denim jacket."

"I don't talk to *blokes*. A bloke is a weirdo who hangs around small children."

"Exactly my point. Who was he? He looked too old to be at school with you."

He shot her a glance. Avery's eyes rolled. "You're giving me Mum vibes."

"I'm just looking out for you, that's all. I didn't like the look of him."

"FreakinhellwhatisYOURproblem?"

How did Avery manage to create single words out of what was normally a sentence? It must be something to do with her flute playing, because she didn't even need to draw breath.

"Who is he?"

"If you must know, he's Zammy's brother's best mate. His name's Duke."

"What's he do for a living?"

"None of your business."

"Tell me."

"He works for a car mechanic, as an apprentice. And for the record, he's really, really nice."

Carts grunted. "He better not be at Zammy's party."

"Or *WHAT?*"

"Or I'll have to rethink whether getting Mum to agree to let you go was the right decision."

Avery's squealed protest pierced his ear. "AreyouforREAL! *A-hole.*"

He winced. "Aves, cut it out. And the rule is I pick you up at 10 pm."

"Noooo! Everyone will think I'm pathetic if I leave at 10."

He prevaricated. "10.30, no later."

"11."

"10.45."

"10.55."

It was time he laid down the rules. "Avery. I'm this close to reneging on the whole deal, and you won't go at all. It's now gone back to 10 pm. No arguing."

She turned the full force of her glare on him. Carts kept his eyes resolutely on the road. He was congratulating himself on winning this one, feeling quite proud of his assertiveness as he drew up at the traffic lights, even thinking he'd make a bloody brilliant parent, when he made the mistake of glancing at her.

Her little nose screwed up.

Then she flipped him the bird.

CHAPTER 9

The phone hadn't stopped all morning.

"Can I offset the cost of my running shoes because I jog to work?"

"What about deducting my takeaway coffees?"

"Can I negatively gear my new campervan? That counts as an investment property, right?"

Then there were the complaints about Ron he had to field.

"Ron hasn't done my last two BAS statements."

"The tax office said Ron hasn't sent through the A240ZB4 form yet."

"Ron NEVER returns my calls…" and on and on.

The only remedy was to leave his desk and make himself another coffee. He wasn't even over the hump of the week. Instead of getting closer, Friday night yoga and seeing Judith seemed to be moving further and further away.

He shouldn't think about the Judith situation. It made him feel like crap.

Instead, he thought about the Avery situation. Which also made him feel like crap, but marginally less so.

Last night's family dinner had not improved on the mall incident.

It had started when Mum remarked on Avery's nails, which were painted in different shades of metallic grey, and she'd turned to Dad and said, "Will you look at her nails, Adrian? They look like she's hit them with a hammer." Silence from Dad. "Can you add your weight to this? Back me up, for once."

Dad glanced over at Avery's hands, then returned to neatly piling mashed potato on his fork. "You're worrying your mother, Avery."

Avery gave them both the stink eye and muttered, "You can divorce your parents, you know."

Carts knew exactly why Avery had grey fingernails. To be honest, he quite liked the one on her thumb, it had a translucent sheen to it. It was meant to match her dress for Saturday. The dress Mum knew nothing about. He sighed and shoved a piece of broccoli into his mouth. Mum looked from his dad to him, clearly exasperated by the lack of male support.

"Okay, what's your opinion, Carter? Surely you don't think it looks nice, do you?"

"I don't mind the one on Ave's thumb so much," he muttered.

Mum glared. Probably she was pissed off because Avery hadn't done her flute practice tonight. If things escalated from here, there would be a stand-off that would do a spaghetti western proud. "C'mon, it's not the end of the world, is it?" he said.

Mum snorted and stabbed at her steak. "If you have to paint your nails, Avery, why can't you stick to a nice normal colour. Like pale pink."

Avery rolled her eyes and slid her elbow along the table, chin cupped on her hand. "What's the point of that?"

"Don't talk back. And sit up straight, you'll get indigestion."

Avery's face looked like a squeezed lemon and Carts flicked back his hair and gave her a warning glare. Avery bit her lower lip and he could see the effort she was making to keep from back-chatting.

To avert disaster, he turned to Dad. "You haven't said how your interview went?"

"Oh, you know, so, so." Dad's brows wrinkled and the wrinkle carried into the smoothness of his bald head. Dad's hair used to be thick and dark like Carts'. Ten years ago, Dad's parents had died in quick succession, and he'd been made redundant from a lecturing position, and his hair all fell out in great big clumps. Now he reminded Carts of a cone-head cartoon, his features disproportionately low in his long head. Alopecia, the doctors had said. He'd even lost his eyebrows, which he'd finally had tattooed on at Mum's insistence.

At least Carts wasn't going to inherit Dad's baldness. All the rest of the Wells men had good thick heads of hair, as his mum would wistfully remark from time to time.

"With it being a new super department, I'm probably not quite dynamic enough." Dad's face turned grim. "I don't fancy my chances against Rodney Fell in Physics, to be honest."

Mum stood up and piled up the plates, and Carts jumped up to help her. "I can always take on more teaching."

"That won't pay the bills, Rosemary," Dad said sadly. "Or for Avery's year in Paris."

"Well, that's not an issue, is it?" Mum said crisply. "At this rate she won't be going anywhere."

A black cloud hovered over Avery's head, but she thankfully kept schtumm and the rest of the evening passed without further mishap.

Taking a slug of strong coffee, Carts realised his stomach was churning with the worry of it all. Or was that the caffeine? It occurred to him that he needed to do something about his stress levels.

Inspiration hit. A mid-week yoga session would be just the ticket.

Usually, he went on Fridays and also attended a class over the weekend. But with taking Judith to dinner his pattern had been messed up.

Back at his desk, he pulled up the yoga timetable on Google.

His eyes widened. Special session Wednesday 6.30–8 pm.

Introduction to Tantra with Fern Bliss.

Tantra? Wasn't that how Sting used to sustain sex for hours?

This could be the answer to his prayers.

Eagerly, he read through the description.

By opening to both our sensual and spiritual being through breathing and awareness of the five senses, we can fulfil our own and our partner's needs more fully. Come and learn the elements of Tantra and how to work with the Chakras to fulfil your sensual and sexual potential.

With Fern Bliss.

He loved Fern's classes. She had a voice that inspired trust and a deep state of subliminal relaxation.

He floated out of her Friday sessions and afterwards, because he was relaxed, he'd been so much better at chatting with Judith than when they were facing each other over a fancy-schmantzy dinner. And the timing was perfect. He'd be able to go home, change and get there no problem, providing he worked his ring off for the rest of the day.

When he arrived at yoga, a few people were gathered on their mats. He scanned the room, because for a moment he worried that Judith might be here too. But she probably didn't need Tantra, did she? Judith clearly knew what she was doing in that department. Christ, that lucky ex of hers—what was wrong with him? Judith had not said much about the split; he guessed they'd grown apart. He knew this guy's loss was his gain, but how the fuck could you ever get tired of kissing Judith?

He was rolling out his mat when Fern glided towards him. "Namaste, Carter," she said with a beatific smile, palms joined in a prayer gesture. "How lovely to see you here."

Carts bowed his head and placed his palms together.

"Namaste Fern. Do I need anything specific for the session?"

"Just the usual props and an open attitude." She studied him. "I think you'll get a lot out of this session, Carter." Her clear blue eyes bathed him in empathy. Fern might be younger than him in years, but she was an old soul. She saw through the masks you hid behind, to the very core of your being. Hopefully, she didn't see *absolutely* everything, he thought as he sat down and crossed his legs in his somewhat bastardised version of the lotus position.

Finally, the candles lit, the scent of incense wafting through the room, Fern sank down on her mat at the front of the room. Her gaze scanned the assembled participants. "Let's OM to get started, shall we?"

Carts closed his eyes, put his palms together and lengthened his spine, imagining a thousand petalled lotus flower rising from the crown of his head.

The resonance of three chanted OMs filled the room.

He let the sound move through him, all his awareness focused on being present in this moment. Slowly he opened his eyes and took in his fellow yogis, all eager and ready to learn.

He felt centred. Peaceful.

"Welcome everyone to tonight's special session." Fern's voice resonated through the room. "Are you ready to explore the magic of Tantra?"

~

JUDITH WAS CLEARING up the occupational therapy department before leaving work when her phone rang. She put a patient's damp papier-mâché pig carefully to one side before locating her phone in her pocket.

"Hi, babe." Pippa's voice bounced down the line. "How's things?"

"Things are…" she forced enthusiasm into her voice, "okay."

"Okay sounds very beige. Are you up for a quick drink?"

"I have my watercolour class, but—"

"Even more beige. Skip it. Come out for a drink instead."

I—oh—" They were going to learn how to "bloom" different colours tonight, but Pippa sounded so excited her phone almost vibrated. Blooming would have to wait.

"I've never known you to be so keen to see me," Judith remarked. "What's going on?"

"Can't I want to spend time with my big sis?"

Judith laughed. "Of course you can."

Truth be told, if it had been Carts asking, she'd happily have skipped every art class under the sun, but although she'd toyed with her phone several times since the weekend, she hadn't plucked up the courage to message and say *how about we meet before Friday*. Images of her failed seduction attempt rotated through her head, a cocktail of confused emotions.

Part of the problem was that the subject of sex had never been discussed in her family. Ever. It wasn't that sex was wrong as such; it was more like it just didn't exist. Dad and Mum never touched, other than a kiss on the cheek, as far as she'd seen. Apparently the three Mellors babies had morphed out of thin air.

And then after Pippa was born, Mum had morphed into thin air too. And when she came back Judith knew she had to be very good and very quiet and never make a fuss or Mum might disappear again.

Love, like sex, was something you had to tread very carefully with.

"Are you still there?" Pippa asked.

"Yes, sorry, I got momentarily distracted."

"Where do you want to meet?"

She thought about the Shamrock and immediately dismissed it. "Oh, I don't know," she said airily. "You choose."

"You know that new place by the Surf Club, Zara's?"

"Oh, yes, that's right next door to where I go to yoga." It seemed there was no way she could escape reminders of Carts.

"I'm meeting someone there around eight," Pippa continued. "So we could get together beforehand."

"Is this a *special* someone?" Judith loaded her voice with nuance.

Pippa merely laughed, rapped out a time and said, "See you there."

So that's how Judith found herself perched on a stool looking out across the manicured lawns of Zara's towards the beach. The Indian Ocean had turned purple as the sun sank onto the horizon like a giant glowing beach ball. Families with sandy feet and happy smiles came up the steps from the beach, joggers ran determinedly along the boardwalk, dogs walked their owners, and cyclists miraculously weaved in between them all without incident.

A young couple sitting on a bench leaned in and kissed. As they got up, the guy flung his arm around the girl's shoulders, the girl reached up and kissed him and they shared a lingering smile before they strolled off.

A bucket of sadness threatened to dump its contents over Judith's head.

How easy love looked. For other people. But before she could start feeling seriously sorry for herself an arm came around her and hugged her hard. "Hey there."

It was Pippa, looking very schmaltzy. She was wearing orange lipstick, and mascara framed her eyes. Pippa in make-up was an almost unseen phenomenon, except for family weddings. That wasn't where it ended either. Her red hair had been cut into a really cute style and she was donned in a silky emerald-green shirt and white slacks.

"You look fantastic," Judith enthused.

"Aw, thanks." Pippa shrugged it off, sat her butt down and reached for her purse.

"What can I get you?"

She seems a little edgy, Judith thought. Edgy, wearing make-up and a funky new hairstyle. Interesting.

"A lemonade…" Heck, she could be more daring than that. "Actually, a glass of bubbles would be great."

"Good one." Pippa jumped up and beelined for the bar. Judith followed her with her eyes. Something *unusual* was definitely going down here.

A short while later they sat at a table in the window and Pippa asked, "Any news on the money?"

Judith took a deep breath. "I went over to his place on Monday night and confronted him."

"And?"

"He owned up to—" she made air quotes, "'borrowing it'."

"Selfish prick."

"I've given him one month to put it back in my account."

"Oh yeah, right. Watch this space. Did he have the grace to tell you why he took it?"

"Not really. He says he's working on some gaming-related project." Even now a warped sense of loyalty stopped her from telling Pippa the whole story, or at least what she knew of it.

"There's all these ways the gaming industry get you to spend more money," Pippa said. "Like paying out for loot boxes that give you an advantage over other players. People can spend thousands on it. It's crazy addictive. I saw a documentary on it the other night. I bet that's what's happened."

"Perhaps." She didn't want to dwell on the possibility he was lying to her as well as stealing from her. His gaming obsession had turned Mark into a shadow person.

"I'm so happy you're out of that relationship."

"So am I."

"And if he doesn't give it back, I'll send the team round."

Judith laughed. The idea of Mark cowering in the corner as The Badassgirls, as Pippa's netball team called themselves, stood over him was quite appealing.

"Thanks Pip. I'll keep you posted." She took another sip of bubbles. "So, what's the new look in aid of?"

"I dunno. I felt like a change." By now Pippa had put most of her lipstick round the rim of the glass and rubbed one eye, which had smudged the mascara.

Judith leaned forward and wiped the mark off Pippa's cheek with a finger. Pippa grinned and slapped her hand away. "Don't," she exclaimed laughingly. Goodness, Pippa was actually blushing!

Judith grinned gleefully. "You *have* got a date tonight, haven't you?"

Pippa shrugged. "Just meeting a friend."

"You've never gone to this trouble for a friend. C'mon, who is it?" Judith wheedled. "One of the footie guys you treat, I bet."

"Don't be daft, you know I can't date patients."

"Ex-patients are okay. Is he hunky?"

Pippa sculled her drink, turning a shade of tomato. "Not saying."

"I'm going to sit here until he arrives."

Pippa shrugged. "Wait as long as you like."

"Aw, stop being so secretive. You're meeting him here, right?"

"Not exactly."

"If you don't tell me, I'll follow you."

"You are so frigging annoying." Pippa started to look flustered. "Maybe we're meeting here. Yes. Happy now?"

Judith snickered and took a mouthful of bubbles, revelling in having the upper hand for once. It didn't happen often, but tonight she really felt like she'd turned the tables on Pippa.

"I'm going to watch through the window and make guesses every time a guy walks past."

She craned her neck. "Is this him...?" She waved her glass towards a man around their age striding towards the entrance. "He's kind of cute."

Pippa thwacked her arm. "Stop it."

But Judith was on a roll. "Oh… this one getting out of his car… look at those shoulders, I bet he plays rugby."

She glanced back at Pippa, who was chewing her lip, her whole face now deep red. "Okay," Pippa huffed, "I guess I've been meaning to t—"

But something else had caught Judith's eye. A group of people who'd clearly just left a yoga session at the surf club, rolled-up mats under their arms as they walked to their cars.

And one, easily a head taller than the rest, tossing dark hair out of his eyes, all loose rangy limbs and angular shoulders, made her heart pound against her ribcage.

Judith's champagne glass hit the table so hard it crashed into a bowl of peanuts, sending them skittering like tiny bullets across the floor.

"Hold that thought," she spluttered. "I'll be straight back." And with that, she flew out the door and after Carts' departing figure.

CHAPTER 10

"*H*i, there."

At his car, wrangling his yoga mat into the back seat, Carts turned and there was Judith, a vision of loveliness, if a little out of breath.

She waved a hand back in the direction she'd come. "I saw you—leaving the surf club." Had she run after him? "I'm not stalking you," pant, "I'm at Zara's next door with my sister."

"Hi, this is a nice surprise." He was quite pleased at how calm he sounded. And when he met her gaze and smiled, it felt like it came straight from his heart chakra.

"I didn't know you did yoga on Wednesdays."

"I don't usually." If Judith looked up the timetable, she'd see that he'd been to a Tantra session, but what the heck, maybe that would go in his favour. "It was a rather stressful day at work, I really needed it."

"Well, I'm glad," she said. "Because I got to see you. Though I'd better just let Pippa know where I am. I kind of dashed off without telling her where I was going." A pause. "You could come and meet her? Would you like to?"

"I'd love to. Will she cope with the yogic vibe?" They both glanced down at his purple yoga pants.

Judith beamed. "Pippa can cope with anything. We're sitting at one of the window tables."

When they entered the restaurant, Judith pointed to a muscular girl with red hair and very bright orange lipstick that almost matched her hair. As he drew closer Carts saw they shared the same ingenuous grey eyes, the only obvious resemblance.

When Judith introduced him, Pippa's face immediately lit up. "Oh, *Carts*. I've heard all about *you*."

Judith squealed, "Pip!" then turned to him. "I haven't been gossiping about you, I promise." "I'd quite like it if you had."

Pippa gave him a cheeky grin. "She hasn't said anything, honest. Just *hinted* there was this guy she had the screaming hots for." He could feel Judith squirm next to him. "She needs a decent boyfriend. The last one was a complete shit."

"Pip-*pa*! We are not—"

"Payback, sis." Pippa rolled her eyes at Carts. "She's been taking the piss out of me for wearing lippy."

"Only because you never do," Judith pointed out. "Oooh, and I see you've reapplied it."

"Shut it." Pippa's foot came out and gave Judith a playful kick. Judith stepped back, laughing.

"My sister teases me too," Carts said.

"Younger or older?" Pippa asked.

"Younger, by fourteen years. And a complete pain in the butt at the moment."

Pippa cocked an eyebrow. "Does she need any tips on how to be an even better pain in the butt?"

"No way!"

"Pip's waiting for her date," Judith said. "And she's being all coy about it."

Pippa shook her head and sculled the rest of her drink.

And then a whole lot of things happened in quick succession. And Carts, having spent the last hour and a half focusing on his five senses, took in every detail. The slender girl with dark hair falling in waves to her shoulders, her lively features brimming with excitement as she scanned the busy restaurant…

The way her eyes lit up when they landed on Pippa.

How Pippa jumped up with an exclamation of "Oh, there's Shaz!" and weaved her way eagerly between the tables.

The way the two women greeted each other, their foreheads almost touching, their smiles sublimely happy… and, of course, he *knew.*

At his side, he heard Judith draw in a sharp breath. She stood, transfixed, eyes wide and unblinking. "Pippa was trying to tell me something earlier," she said after a moment. "And now I get it was really, really important."

"I FEEL SO *AWFUL.*"

Carts had slowed his step to prolong the walk to their cars when Judith's words made him glance at her. A tight little frown knitted her brow. "How could I not know? She's my *sister.*"

"Sometimes things hide in plain sight," he said. "Even more so, I reckon, when we're close to someone."

"That's so true." Her lips quirked ruefully. "They look so perfect together. And so happy. I can't believe I didn't twig, Pippa always talked about this girl in the netball team, how amazing a player she is. I thought that was just Pip, she's so enthusiastic. I missed the signs. I've missed them for years."

"Like what?"

"Like how she'd change the subject whenever I asked about boyfriends. And she always refers to guys as knuckleheads and douchebags."

"She's right. We are." Carts thought about the countless nights wiping himself out at the pub with Aaron and Dan. Yep. Utter douchebags.

"I just assumed she hadn't met the right guy… like, how one-eyed can you get?" She groaned and tapped her forehead with the heel of her hand. "Here I am thinking I'm this cool *woke* person and I just assumed… urkkkk, I am so *ashamed* of myself."

He laughed gently. "You're just like me."

"In what way?"

"You take too much responsibility for other people's happiness."

"Oh, you do that?" A moment's pause. "It feels like I've really let her down, that she couldn't talk to me…"

"Maybe she wasn't ready to."

"Maybe…" They'd reached her little red hatchback and she turned and leaned her back against the door, smiling up at him. "And thanks."

"For what?"

"Listening to me angsting. And being so cool and calm about the whole thing."

He gave her a perplexed look. "Why would I be any other way?"

She hesitated. "I don't know. Except… Mark was always so judgemental, I guess. He has a tolerance quota that's—" she squeezed her forefinger and thumb almost together, "this big."

Carts decided Pippa's summation was right. He did sound like an A-grade prick.

"I've been too forgiving over the years," Judith continued on a sigh. "His dad left when he was small and his mum brought him up and worked three jobs to keep them afloat. I always make excuses for that… he wouldn't be like this if blah blah hadn't happened."

"Everyone has tough things happen in their past." He felt a prickle of envy that she should still care enough about this guy's feelings to defend him. "Eventually we all have to accept we're an adult and take responsibility for our actions."

She sighed. "I get that more than you can imagine." She leaned her back against the door of her car and the evening breeze whipped gossamer tendrils across her face. She peeled them back, strand by strand, with her fingers. How he loved all the tiny details of her. Precious, and committed to memory.

"Talking to you has really helped. I'd have gone home and kept beating myself up about this, but now… I feel easier."

His scalp prickled with the compliment. "Thank you."

"No, thank *you*. I really like that we're getting to know each other better, you know, at a deeper level."

"Me too." It was impossible not to notice how enticing her lips were, even though he was really focused on her mind right now. "Guess I'll see you Friday evening at yoga, then."

"Yes, of course." She rummaged in her bag for her keys. He kept his distance; he couldn't risk another chin to head bump. She found them and then lifted her face. Suddenly he was drowning in the misty softness of her eyes. The messages from his chakras scrambled into one hot mess somewhere in the region of his groin. He tried to move the energy higher, into his heart, not his freakin' dick, but his body had other ideas. Should he kiss her, not kiss her? Cheek? Lips? *Shite*.

Then Judith said, "Would you like to come to dinner tomorrow night?"

"That's Thursday?"

"Yes, tomorrow is Thursday." She cocked her head. "Unless you have something else on?"

"You mean, just me and you?" Expectations crammed into his head. His breathing went haywire.

Her lips quirked. "Do you have a problem with that?"

"No!" It came out way too loud. "Nada. Zilch." Now she looked puzzled, and he rushed on. "As in, no problem." he took a breath. *Slow down, man.* "What I meant is, I'd love to."

"Great, because I bought this Ottolenghi recipe book a while back... at the Book Genie actually."

"What?"

"Ottolenghi. He's a famous chef in London. No-one in my family likes trying new recipes much, so... Do you like Turkish-influenced food?"

"Er, you mean kebabs?"

She laughed. "How about babaganoush?"

"Baba-gan-do anything for you," he said jauntily, then grimaced. "Sorry, that was a crap line. What is it?"

"It's a baked eggplant dip. I thought I'd make it as part of a meze platter."

He hadn't got a clue what that was either, but after his last atrocious line, he'd play it safe. "I'm salivating already."

Judith beamed; he was sure she guessed he was way out of his depth when it came to culinary issues.

"I'll text you my address. Around sevenish?"

"Perfect."

She leaned in and kissed him on the lips, so swiftly he had no time to react.

"And for the record, I really love your bad jokes."

CHAPTER 11

*CW*hoever said women were great at multi-tasking was a liar, Judith thought as she dashed from the bathroom towards the smell of burning eggplant. She'd decided after work that following the recipe by oven baking them would take way too long. So she'd pan-fried them instead.

All very well, until you forgot you'd left the heat on high while washing your hair.

She flicked off the gas, and after twisting a towel tightly round her head, flipped the eggplant slices out of the pan with a spatula. They were salvageable. After all, wasn't babaganoush meant to taste smoky?

Smoky, not burnt to a cinder.

She took a big breath and squeezed her eyes shut. *Okay Judith, one thing at a time. Leave the eggplant to cool. Go dry your hair. Then come back and finish off the meze platter. There's still fifty-five minutes until he arrives. You've got this.*

She had to smile. She'd talked herself through things ever since she was a child. Her very first day of school, her inoculations, all the times when she'd sat alone eating her lunch in a corner of the playground. Pretending she had her very own fairy godmother sitting on her shoulder.

Yeah, she might be sensible on the outside, but deep inside, secretly, she did believe in fairy tales with happily ever afters.

Back in the bathroom she blow-dried her hair into soft waves and thought about how she seemed to be the one initiating most of the kisses. Like Sleeping Beauty in reverse. But if Polly was right, then... maybe... oh, the poor darling. They were really on a par, weren't they?

Because sex had barely been on the agenda with Mark for the past couple of years.

Rusty. Totally out of practice. Her lady bits put into cold storage, but clearly, all it took was a couple of kisses with Carts and everything was suddenly wide awake and ready for action. Slicking mousse into her hair, she grinned as a glob of fluff caught in the front. It reminded her of that scene in—what was the movie? Where the hair gel wasn't gel at all...

She brushed her hair harder.

It was almost exactly fifty-five minutes to the second when the doorbell rang. Like a *MasterChef* contestant, she arranged the finished platter on the table. It all looked so beautiful, the babaganoush whipped and smooth and scattered with parsley from her little garden, next to a vivid purple beetroot dip and flatbreads. And the lamb tagine she'd prepared and popped in the slow cooker before she left for work, now giving off rich aromas of tomatoes and rosemary.

She took off her apron and smoothed down the second dress she'd bought on her shopping binge. This one was pale blue, dotted with daisy sprigs with tiny fabric-covered buttons all the way up the front. Only the top five actually undid, the rest were for show. If it got to the unbuttoning stage, she'd... *Judith*. Stop, just *stop*. Scooting down the hall, she sucked in her cheeks to hold back a telltale grin, but nothing would stop the excitement fizzing like champagne bubbles in her stomach as she flung open the front door.

And then... there he was.

Tall, dark and gorgeous, handing her a gigantic bunch of red roses. Real roses! "For you," he said.

Mark had only ever stretched to carnations. Once. Under duress, when she'd complained five years into their relationship that he'd never bought her flowers.

She wasn't going to actually count, but she reckoned there were a dozen.

She felt the caress of his dark eyes on her face as she stuffed her nose into the bunch of roses.

"Wow, thank you." The smile she'd been trying to contain streamed out in all directions. "These are beautiful."

The return flash of his teeth sent the blood rushing to her head.

Then he ducked his head and entered.

CARTS SAT BACK with a big sigh. "You know that line about the way to a guy's heart is through his stomach... well... if it wasn't such a cliché—"

"I'll accept the cliché if there's a genuine compliment attached."

He met her eyes, drowned a little, resurfaced. "That is the best meal I've had in years."

"Thank you." She dimpled. "Is there a corner left for dessert?"

"Ah, there's always a dessert corner. Don't you find that kind of strange? You can be full up to your earlobes, but there's always that bit of space left for something sweet."

"Yeah, the sweet spot." Their eyes snagged again, held for a beat longer. Make no mistake, she kept hitting his sweet spot. All evening, watching her at the stove, smoothly juggling all the components of preparing and serving a meal. And okay, yes, he'd let himself indulge in some romantic fantasies; Judith with a kid against her hip, stirring a pot on the stove—he pulled himself up short—amend that image, *he'd* be stirring the pot and *she'd* be sitting nursing the baby... except he'd freakin' have to learn to cook first. Or maybe *he'd* be feeding the baby, but then, Judith might be breastfeeding so it would depend on the age of their baby. And shite, babies meant overcoming a few hurdles first. His palms went clammy.

He wasn't even thinking of staying over.

No pressure, no pressure, no pressure.

Since yesterday he'd unwound about the whole sex thing. He'd lain in bed in the dark, and practised Fern's techniques. When he'd relived the kissing episode and his groin had predictably lit up like a Christmas tree, he'd breathed and visualised a deep red glow at the base of his spine. He'd let the heat radiate through his pelvis, but only so much, stopping it before the glow turned into a full-blown flame.

Finally, he'd drifted off to sleep.

Naturally, he'd woken up with a stonking morning glory, but that was beyond his control, so he'd accepted it, with kindness. He couldn't be responsible for controlling his dick in his sleep, after all.

He'd fixed things in the shower, not in a frenzied, desperate way, but breathing evenly, eyes closed as he leaned against the tiles, feeling every drop of warm water on his skin and imagining Judith's fingers exploring his body until the waves crashed through him, leaving his knees weak, but his mind clear.

All day at work he'd felt remarkably calm and centred.

"Where did you learn to cook so well?" he asked now.

"I started young."

"Your mum taught you?"

"I kind of taught myself." Her lips tightened for a second. "Mum had bad postnatal depression after Pippa was born."

He hadn't expected that. "Cripes. How old were you?"

"I was seven and Luke was three. Mum was in hospital for a while with Pip on a mother-baby unit. I used to feel so proud when I helped get Luke's tea ready. Nothing major, just peanut butter sandwiches at first. Dad would cut up the carrot and celery, and I'd arrange them like a smiley face on the plate with his sandwiches."

"That must have been tough on you."

"Not really, I loved doing it. I guess cooking became my way of showing I care." Her face lit up. "Dad gave me this cookery book as a birthday present, a kids' one, with easy recipes. I've still got it; for you know… if I have kids one day." She rushed on, "Anyway, I made most of the recipes out of it. Jam drops, macaroni cheese, chocolate brownies…" She picked at the edge of a table mat, her face pensive, and he badly wanted to reach over and take her hand.

"How long did you get your brother's tea for?"

"Oh, a couple of months maybe. I don't exactly remember because I still helped out when Mum came home. She spent a lot of time in her dressing gown. And I would rock Pippa to sleep and play with her to stop her crying. Mum couldn't stand the crying." She looked up and huffed out a laugh. "Honestly, I don't think I ever felt like a kid. I was so worried about everyone." She got up and picked up his plate. "Hardly surprising I ended up in a helping profession."

"I get that." Carts stood up too. "I only went into accounting because I was good at maths. Wish I'd been more artistic, like you, but there you are, I'm just a boring number cruncher."

She turned to him as he handed her some dishes.

"There's nothing wrong with that. I'd love to understand maths better. But you're so much more than a number cruncher."

"Really. In what way?"

"You're highly intuitive."

Carts scoffed, went back to the table and started clearing the condiments. "I don't think many people would agree with you."

"Well, they're wrong. I can tell by the way you talk about your sister, and your friends. How you were last night with Pippa and Shaz."

Flustered, he muttered, "I—I care. That's all."

"That's everything."

Inside he glowed, but he couldn't manage to say a plain and simple thank you, so he grabbed hold of the segue as he put the salt and pepper shakers on the bench. "Talking of Pippa… have you spoken to her since last night?"

"I've tried to call her all day. She texted just before I left work saying she's been super busy and she hopes I liked Shaz and that I understood, to which I replied of course I do, one hundred and ten per cent. I did start to write I was sorry for not being there for her, but after what you said, I stopped myself. I've thought about it and you're right, Pip probably wasn't ready to share before now." She came back to the table and filled up their wine glasses. He watched her fingers curl around the bottle, and remembered how wonderful her hand had felt holding his. "Our family have never talked about it… sex and all that related stuff."

He took the glass from her and sat down. "Mine are the same. Mum still acts like Avery is ten years old. And my dad's only comfortable talking sex if it involves two-celled animals dividing. I have an intimate knowledge of the reproductive cycle of the amoeba, thanks to Dad."

"That sounds exciting." Judith took a seat opposite him. "I think my parents expected school would take care of it." She giggled. "But our sex ed was useless. Mrs Bendigo, who the boys all called Mrs Bendover, ran a couple of sessions. I remember watching a movie with close-ups of a sperm fertilising an egg, and some horrible pictures of venereal diseases. She left handouts at the front of the class about how saying no to sex was the only safe sex."

He snorted. "Oh Christ, yeah, don't remind me. We had a guy called John Prior, with a terrible high-pitched laugh who got everyone stretching condoms over bananas. They were all around the school grounds for days afterwards." Carts had found one hung on his locker with a note saying, "You won't need this, stick dick." No way was he going to tell Judith that.

"Eweey, that's enough to put you off dessert. Talking of which, I almost forgot." She jumped up, went to the fridge and brought out two crystal glass bowls. "Chocolate orange mousse—wait." Her head dived into the fridge again, and when she turned around she brandished a can of whipped cream. "This was the only cream they had left at the IGA."

At which they both burst out laughing.

Sure, it was childish, Carts thought as they made crazy swirls on top of their chocolate mousse and wiped tears of laughter out of their eyes, but there was something cathartic about discussing his childhood with Judith in a way he'd never talked about it before.

The ambient background music stopped and suddenly the sound of their spoons scraping their dishes was inordinately loud. Judith got up and went over to her phone. "What would you like to listen to?"

Why not admit it. "I'm a huge fan of eighties music. I collect vintage LPs."

"Wow, really? There's something so romantic about records isn't there?"

"Yeah, that magic circle of black vinyl. You hold it in your hands, dust it down, place it on the turntable. It's a ritual. And then you sit back, and the music sounds so much better. It's a whole body/mind thing."

Judith glanced up from checking out Spotify. "What's your favourite band from the eighties?"

"Don't make me choose. The early eighties was a revolutionary time, punk rock, the New Romantics, bands like Ultravox—have you heard 'Vienna'?"

She shook her head.

"Oh, man, have you a treat in store. You have to sit in a dark room, smoking Gauloises cigarettes—I don't smoke, but if I did I'd be puffing away at a Gauloises—and look deep and brooding."

She laughed. "I can see it now. I really love the boppy eighties songs and the look—all that fluffy hair and shimmery blue eyeshadow. Oooh, remember Madonna's pointy tits?" She tapped her chin, her cheeks pinking up. "'Like a Virgin'. And there's another I loved... 'Manic Monday', who wrote that one?"

"The Bangles. They were such an underrated band. Their album, *Different Light* was an absolute classic."

"You know so much about music. Do you play an instrument like Avery?"

"Nah, but I mime well. I do a fantastic guitar solo of Mark Knopfler. It's my party piece."

"I didn't see you perform it at your thirtieth."

He coughed into his fist. "Yeah, well, I didn't want to make an idiot of myself in front of someone special."

"It would really impress *someone* in this room if you did a rendition now."

Bashful, he bit his lip.

"Oh come on," she teased. "I've always found Mark Knopfler kind of sexy to be honest."

So of course, that was Carts' cue to do his rendition of Mark Knopfler, hair flopping over his eyes as he mimed the words to "Money for Nothing" on an imaginary guitar in perfect synch to the music. He stopped halfway through a chord, flicked his fringe out of his eyes and said, "You know Sting was in this, don't you?"

"Really?"

"Yeah, listen, I'll play it again." He replayed it and they both listened intently. "Hear that? At the start, the high notes—that's Sting."

"Oh yes, I can hear him now." She looked wistful. "My all-time favourite song of Sting's is 'Fields of Gold'. Was that written in the eighties?"

"No, it was released in 1993."

She giggled, "I can't believe you know that."

"Accountant brain, good with numbers," he muttered with a sheepish grin.

"Do you like it?"

"Do I what! I tear up every time I hear it. I don't know why but it always hits me right—" he pressed a curled fist to his chest, "in here."

He cast her a quick glance but saw nothing but admiration in her eyes. A woman, finally, who didn't judge him when he admitted he cried. Though he might have to know her better before he fessed up to shedding tears the first time he watched *ET*.

"Let's play it." Her eyes shone and he knew he'd go to the end of the earth to keep that light alive in her eyes.

They found it on Spotify, their heads close together and their breaths mingling, and then somehow, he was not quite sure how exactly, they were standing facing each other in the middle of the room, and it seemed the easiest thing for his arm to slide around her waist, and her head to rest on his shoulder.

As Sting's voice crooned over the speakers, the beauty of the lyrics choked him up.

A feather-light kiss landed on his neck. Then another.

Heat rolled through him like a summer storm.

Down below, the beast stirred.

She raised her head and for a long moment their gazes fused before Carts lowered his head and sought her lips. And it occurred to him that he could fight this, or he could give in. He gave in, and in seconds their kisses had turned passionate.

They landed with a thud and a laugh on the sofa, their legs and arms awkwardly tangled and after a moment, when he'd accidentally jabbed her in the chin with his elbow, Judith suggested they might be more comfortable on the floor. So, he grabbed a few cushions and put them under her head and lay down next to her.

He watched, mesmerised, as she undid the buttons of her dress one by one. "They only go this far," she murmured, pointing to just below her breastbone. Then she took his hand and slid it inside her dress.

It had been so long since Carts had touched a woman's breasts, and even longer since he'd actually felt they wanted him to, but there was no mistaking Judith's reaction as she arched into him with a moan and pushed her pebbled nipple into his touch.

The beast was now fully awake and threatening to burst out of its cage.

A wave of panic spread into his scalp as the throb in his groin intensified.

And then he remembered something Fern had said during her Tantra session.

Focus on your partner's pleasure.

If he gave everything to Judith in this moment, thought of nothing but the joy of giving her pleasure, then… maybe, he could control his body's crazy reactions.

Maybe he could tame the beast.

With a ragged sigh, he bent his head to her breast and sucked her nipple into his mouth. She let out a soft mewl of pleasure.

Summoning the energy from his base chakra, vertebrae by vertebrae, Carts raised it to his heart chakra. Slowing the pace even further, he circled her nipple with his tongue.

Another moan and her hands tangled in his hair.

Yes. He could—he *could* do this.

He just had to focus all his energy on making sweet love to Judith.

"This is all for you," he whispered. "Just tell me what you want."

CHAPTER 12

*J*udith's head fell back against the cushions as sensations washed through her in delicious waves.

She wanted to get closer, to push her thigh between his and crazily rip off both their clothes simultaneously, but she seemed transfixed by his mouth teasing her nipple. As for words, all that came out was a sigh of "ah—ohhh" as an insistent throb started up in a place much lower down. The more Carts sucked and licked her nipple the more her power of speech deserted her. She tried to communicate with her body, pressing herself against him, but it seemed every time she did he pulled away a fraction.

A tiny seed of doubt penetrated her euphoria.

But then he said in a low, husky tone, "Tell me what you want," and that cracked her wide open.

"Down—lower—please," she gasped.

He glanced up from the swell of her exposed breast, his eyes glinting behind a devilish lock of hair. "How much lower?"

"Um—a bit."

"Show me." He slid his hand down the front of her dress until he got to the fake buttons, which made her moan with frustration. She flapped her hand wildly in the direction of her legs.

"I could always take a different approach," he suggested huskily. "Like come from below, maybe."

"I think—yes, maybe that would be best."

"I'll do anything you want." Throatier, with emphasis. "I mean, *anything.*"

Oh heavens. He was offering her a feast of pleasure. Could she? Ask for the *one* thing Mark had never been that into, the only thing that could guarantee her release. And oh, she *wanted that.*

White-hot lust surged through her body.

"This…" With feverish fingers, she ruched up her skirt and let her thighs fall open. He made a sound of assent, a deep grunt she could somehow tell was full of awe and appreciation. Suddenly confident, she clasped his shoulders and guided his body down hers until he was kneeling between her thighs.

Gentle kisses ranged along her inner thigh, one by one, circling higher and higher. "Am I getting warm?"

"Uh-huh."

"Warmer?"

"Mmmmmm!"

The sudden gentle pressure on her clitoris made her practically levitate out of her body. All he'd done, she realised, was press the pad of his tongue on her over her panties. She groaned her encouragement.

He sucked her over the top of her panties, and it had to be the most erotic sensation she'd ever experienced. Rainbows of colour gathered behind her eyelids. She needed more and it couldn't wait. Barely able to think, she took his hand and guided it under the gusset of her panties. He kissed her fingers and everything was hot and steamy and musky scented as she felt the tug when he moved the little morsel of fabric aside.

And then, oh, oh, oh… the lap of his tongue between her folds, rhythmic, firm, and so utterly perfect until she was writhing with delight. She had to pull a cushion onto her chest and hug it tight because she didn't have him to hug tight, because, well… *obviously,* he was down there working… *wonders.*

Then he slipped a finger inside her.

99

"Oh—OH—HOT!" She hadn't realised she'd said it out loud until she felt the vibration of his laugh against her labia and then... he blew on her, right there, where the sensation was most intense.

God help her...

And now he was sucking again, alternating with that shaft of warmth as he blew...

back and forth until—

Hips rocking, Judith bit down on that darn cushion so hard as her orgasm gathered force. But when she came, there was no way to stop the words spilling out of her mouth in a garble of "oh my God", and "Cart-errrrr!!!"

For a while, she could only lie limp and panting, staring at the decorative plaster rose in the centre of the ceiling and wondering why she'd never noticed how beautiful it was before.

But then he was removing the cushion from her hands and kissing her gently on the lips.

Looking down, one breast, the smaller one, peeped out and she could see his wistful look as he gently pulled her dress back over it.

What? He wasn't taking this any further...

"You...?" she asked, incredulous.

He smiled, shook his head. "But, but... I want to give back to you." Bewildered, she pushed up on her elbow and looked at him.

"We will. I promise. Just not now..." He took her fingers and again kissed each one in turn.

"B—but I want to do the same—to give you..."

Yet even as she said it a soporific heaviness was overcoming her senses. Her limbs leaden, her brain delightfully befuddled.

"Very soon. Just not tonight."

Judith roused herself. "If it's to do with no condom. I could—"

"Shsssh—" A finger came to his lips. "I'm going to put you to bed then leave you to sleep."

With effort, she tried to protest again. "Ohh, no-no-no-no. Stay, pleaaasssse."

"I'll stay for a while."

"You can't drive," she pleaded. "We drank the whole bottle of wine, you'll be over the limit."

He hesitated, stroking the damp hair away from her forehead, his eyes full of tenderness. "Okay, I'll lie with you."

She was so sleepy as he put her to bed, barely able to focus. Like a rag doll, she let him peel off her dress and when he pulled back the covers, she sank thankfully down on the mattress. When she felt him spoon into her back and his arms fold around her, she relaxed with a happy sigh.

"It's an extra-long mattress," she murmured sleepily. "Plenty of leg room."

"Perfect," he whispered, and she felt his lips on the soft skin just below her ear.

"Do you like me?" she mumbled drowsily. The question was unnecessary really, after what Carts had just gifted her; some last vestige of insecurity.

All she heard before slumber took her were the words, "More than you can ever imagine."

As CARTS WALKED, a gentle rain pattered onto his head and shoulders. The night was balmy, embracing him in a mist that was unusual for Perth in late summer, when usually the air was hot and dry. He lifted his face up to the sky and saw the moon, shadowy and soft behind a veil of clouds.

He felt wonderful, alive—more than alive. Like every cell in his body was vibrating with cosmic energy.

He'd given everything he had to pleasuring Judith, and sure, he'd been aroused (how could he not be), but not to the point where it was out of his control.

Every time he'd got close to the edge, he'd directed the energy back upwards into his heart and given it all to Judith. With every ounce of his being he'd focused on her body's response, the pulse and rhythm of her build-up and release.

He'd always known that if he couldn't attract a woman easily, he had to have other skills, and yeah, even when girls didn't dig him that much, they always told him he was really good at getting them off.

It just seemed he could never quite win their hearts.

Until now.

The realisation that Judith wanted him as much as he wanted her blew him away. It almost overwhelmed him that he could inspire such strong desire in a woman. Here was a completely different image from the one he'd always had of himself. The guy who never quite made the grade. Like a bird with a damaged wing. He might be able to fly, but he'd always be a bit crooked and prone to ungainly landings.

But now he was soaring on the wings of an eagle. In the slipstream, gliding effortlessly.

The Proclaimers song, *I'm Gonna Be* suddenly sprang into his head.

Because he would, wouldn't he? He'd walk 500 miles for her, wear the soles off his shoes, worship at her feet. Give her everything he had.

Which was probably why he didn't realise that he'd walked not towards his townhouse in the city, but towards his parents' rambling art deco home.

He almost laughed as he found himself on their street.

Judith's house was in the neighbouring suburb; he guessed it was an easy enough error to make.

He sneaked round the back to where the spare key was always kept under a flower pot and groped around until he felt the cold metal of the key that opened the french doors to the music room.

Once inside, he tiptoed through the dimly lit room, making out the familiar shapes of the piano, of Avery's flute stand in a corner, the scents of the house more intense in the darkness. They'd eaten Mum's bolognese earlier; he could detect the smell of the herbs and spices she used.

He made his way up the stairs, carefully stepping over the one that creaked. His room, he knew, would be the same as when he'd left four years ago: the bed made up, a few knick knacks on the shelf, along with a photo of his university graduation; him a skinny beanpole with Mum and Dad smiling proudly at his side and Avery missing her two front teeth. It was as if Mum hoped he'd come back home one day. Never quite accepting he was an adult. Was that Mum's problem now with Avery? Not wanting her baby to grow up and go out into the world?

As he made his way along the landing he paused outside Avery's room. The door was partially open, so he slipped inside.

He could hear the steady low rasp of her breath, see the hump of her silhouette in the bed, and, caught in a beam of light from the street lamp outside, her hair splayed out on the pillow like a dark river.

He tiptoed closer, holding his breath.

Her thumb hovered around her mouth, the tip at her lips and he knew that even now, it would slide into her mouth at times.

Just like when she was a baby.

And then he saw Mutsy's ear sticking up from under the covers.

She was cuddling dear old Mutsy.

That gesture struck him as so achingly beautiful, so utterly vulnerable. And suddenly the thought of her prancing off in that silver scrap of material tomorrow night froze him to the spot; he totally got why Mum was paranoid about it.

Avery was so innocent.

So oblivious to the mess of navigating this shit-show called growing up.

For Christ's sake, he was thirty and he still couldn't fathom the whole love thing out. Avery still had the war zone to work through, all the hurts and rejections to overcome.

A visceral pain constricted his chest. He hoped to God she'd work it out before she got to his age.

Gently, he reached out and curled the cover around battered old Mutsy. Two button eyes stared back, round and bemused, as if poor old Mutsy was constantly puzzled by the vagaries of life.

He patted Mutsy's ear.

"Wouldn't be young again for quids, eh Mutsy?" he whispered.

It seemed to Carts like those button eyes spelled their agreement.

Bending down, he dropped a kiss on Avery's apple-scented hair before tiptoeing out of the room.

CHAPTER 13

*S*omething soft tickled Judith's nose, followed by a heady, sweet scent. Was she still dreaming? And if so, why had her dream taken her into a florist's shop? She cracked open an eyelid to be met by a soft, deep red hue. Opened the other and blinked until the object came into focus.

A red rose. On her pillow.

She sat up abruptly as memories of the night before flooded in and warmth simultaneously flooded her body, followed by a cold snap of reality as she realised the coverlet was neatly smoothed over the other side of the bed.

Carts had not stayed the night.

But there was a rose. And next to it, a note.

She pushed the hair out of her eyes, unfolded the lined piece of paper torn from her shopping notepad in the kitchen.

Thank you for the most beautiful evening.

You filled my senses.

See you at yoga tonight.

Carts xxx

She heard a sound and realised she'd let out a big sigh. Sudden tears blurred her vision. No man had ever said anything so romantic to her before. He'd gifted her his lips, his tongue, worshipped her body like she was Venus de Milo.

And taken nothing in return.

Sinking back into the pillow, she relived the pleasure of his touch, her fingers tracing dreamily down her breasts, to her nipple, caressing it briefly before moving across the soft swell of her belly and down…

She could honestly go all over again. Right now. Her eyes went hazy, recalling that dark head moving between her legs, administering such… her fingers found the soft curls, the swollen secret spot…

Her phone rang.

She snatched her hand back with a sheepish smile.

"Sis!"

"Pip"

"Are you at work?

"No, why—I mean," she cast a look at the clock on the bedside table and then, horrified, threw back the covers.

"Oh my God, it's 8.30!"

"Yeah, I know. What's the problem?"

"I'm still in bed and I have our team meeting—like, NOW." She'd never been late for work before. God, what a couple of years of pent-up orgasms could do to your sleep patterns. (Self-pleasure had nothing on Carts' gold medal performance.)

She scrunched the phone against her ear, bounced off the bed and ran around to her clothes drawer, grabbing knickers and a bra before dashing into the bathroom.

"Are you alright?" Pippa asked.

"Yes, never better, and Pip—Shaz is so lovely. I am so happy for you."

"Isn't she freakin' amazing?"

"Absolutely. You got all my messages, didn't you?"

"Yes, and sorry I didn't call you back yesterday. Work was crazy and then we had dinner with Shaz's parents. And guess what? We've decided to move in together!"

"That's wonderful!"

"Which is why I have to tell Dad and Mum."

"Absolutely!" Judith turned the shower on full blast.

"Tonight."

"Tonight!" This was sudden even by Pippa's standards. "Maybe you shouldn't spring this on them quite so soon. I mean, you know Mum isn't that good with..."

"With what?" Judith watched the steam as it fogged up the mirror. "Go on say it." Pip's voice was suddenly strained.

"Things that are..."

"Deviant? Warped? is that what you mean?"

"No! of course not. I mean, things that are outside of her life experience."

"That's the litmus test, is it? Mum's experience of life. If we went by her experience, we'd all be sent to hell for masturbating."

Crikey, that was a close call, considering where her fingers had been heading when Pippa rang.

"How long are you going to make excuses for her?" Pippa demanded.

"I'm not." Judith tested the water gushing out of the shower head and nearly burnt her fingers. Turned on the cold tap. "I just understand that her childhood was difficult and—"

"Honestly, right now, I don't care about Mum's childhood. That's not my problem. Shaz and I discussed it after you'd left; the time is right. We've been dating for six months and now I've told you, that's it, no more hiding in the shadows. The rest of the fam needs to know."

"I get that."

Pippa bowled on, barely drawing breath. "So listen, I've organised a table at Harry Tan's. I've asked Luke and Kirsty to come too. Harry's booked us the private room."

"Oh, right, so everyone."

"Yep, and Shaz will be holding my hand. I'm shouting our love to the whole fucking world. Actually, Harry already knows. We've been going there for Peking duck ever since we started dating." A pause for breath. "Look babe, I need to practise what I'm going to say or I'm bound to shout at Mum. Can we catch up beforehand?"

Wham! Wham! *Wham!* There was so much to take in, her head was reeling. There went her plans for yoga. And seducing Carts afterwards.

Judith gulped down her disappointment. But her sister needed her by her side now, probably more than at any other time.

"Of course I can. When... where?"

"Straight after work. At Glide. I'll make sure I'm quick with my last patient."

"I'll be there," Judith said firmly.

After Pip had declared undying love and appreciation and hung up, Judith stepped into the shower. Thoughts yapped at the periphery of her brain, but she knew there was no time to let them in because if she didn't rush, Dr Jonathon Pritchard, Echidna Ward's head psychiatrist (aka Dr Death, aptly named by Polly because of his morbidly pale skin and morose stare) would make toast of her in front of the whole team.

She made it into work in record time. Dr Death's familiar drone met her ears as she hurried towards the staff meeting room. Quaking in her shoes, she finally summoned the courage to click the latch and push the door open.

The room looked haphazard. Polly lounged on one elbow at the far end of the table, sucking on the top of her pen. Her lips looked chafed, and she was wearing a bright yellow dress with poppies on it more suited to a summer party, incongruently paired with a black leather jacket that was way too big for her.

Solo's short dark hair spiked more than usual, and a dreamy smile played around his lips.

There was an energy that was palpable.

It was the same kind of energy she sensed she was giving off. What Polly would call "right royally fucked". Except she hadn't been fucked exactly...

She slipped into her chair with a mumbled apology.

Dr Death stopped talking and looked around the room, an exasperated pull to his thin lips.

"Would anyone like to explain why you were all late this morning?"

After the team meeting, Judith scurried into the occupational therapy storeroom and quickly dialled Carts' number.

When he picked up, she had to sit down, her knees went so wobbly at the sound of his voice.

"It's you," she managed weakly.

"And it's you." She died a little at the warmth in his voice, then blurted, "I'm really sorry, I can't make yoga tonight."

She felt the energy change on the other end.

"Oh, right."

"Pippa's arranged to tell our whole family tonight. About being gay. She's bringing Shaz. And I need to be there to make sure it goes okay."

"Yes, of course you do." It was genuine, but she could hear his disappointment.

"We could meet Saturday—maybe?" she supplied breathlessly.

A pause. "It's this party thing of Avery's. I'm kind of on big brother duty."

"All night?" She rubbed at her constricted throat.

"Until ten." A pause. "But we could, er, we could meet after, if you wanted."

"Oh, yes! I've got a sewing project I can get on with and then... then you could come round to my place?"

"That'd be great. But I wouldn't get there until around 10.45, if that's not too late."

"Never too late." She knew she was blushing. "I'll have a nightcap ready."

"Sounds perfect."

Her cheeks on fire now, she managed, "And thank you for... the rose... and—everything else." How did you thank someone for the most intense orgasm of your life? "Oh, Polly's here. I have to go."

She heard him laugh softly before saying a quick goodbye. She tucked her phone into her pocket as Polly advanced into the storeroom, hugging the bulky leather jacket around her chest.

"Good time last night?" The way Polly said it and the accompanying smirk made Judith feel like she had been initiated into a special club; but that was silly, because how on earth would Polly know what happened last night?

She tried for a casual shrug. "I overslept."

"Sure, you did." Polly gave a throaty laugh.

"Anyway, I have a group in ten minutes, and I've got to prepare soooo—" Judith kept bustling around, grabbing tubes of paint and brushes. "Is there any other reason you're here other than to gloat that I was late for work for the first time ever?"

Polly advanced. "Do you have a spare coverall I could borrow? I need to return this jacket to its owner and I can't walk around—" she flung the jacket wide and showed off her glorious cleavage in the low-cut summer dress "—with my tits hanging out all day. Not exactly appropriate at work."

"I'll try and find you something." Judith avoided eye contact.

She sensed Polly's green gaze lasering into her back as she checked through her apron collection. "Did Carts stay with you last night?"

"Kind of—not really."

"Is that a problem?"

"No— no, not at all. I mean, yes, sort of—" She felt her shoulders droop, suddenly overwhelmed.

"Do you need to workshop this over a coffee later?"

She was going to say no, hold it all in like she always did, but then she looked into Polly's warm, concerned eyes.

And she knew that Polly was the one person who could advise her on her next move.

"Yes, yes I do." She nodded fervently.

"Great, meet you at eleven in the staff canteen. And thanks for this." Polly ripped off the jacket, stuck her arms in the coverall and fastened it with the tie around her waist. "How do I look?"

If Judith had been Polly she'd have said, "Like a well-fucked woman." But she wasn't, so she beamed and said, "Lovely."

As Polly walked out, one of the patients, Esme, chortled. "Love the look, Polly. Are you helping run art therapy today?"

"No, Esme, it's my new boho chic social worker uniform." Polly grinned and sashayed off, her yellow dress swishing beneath the hem of the paint-stained coverall.

Judith turned back into the storeroom. The leather jacket was looped over a stool where Polly had left it. She examined it. Thick black leather. A biker's jacket. As she flipped back the collar, she saw a name, scrolled in texta on the label.

Solo Jakoby.

Judith grinned her head off.

An hour and a half later she took the lift to the eighth floor, located Polly sitting in the far corner of the staff canteen and, strolling over, dropped the jacket onto the chair next to her.

"You left this behind." She quirked an eyebrow in what she thought was a very good rendition of Polly. Polly tossed her head but a smile played around her lips. And a stray curl bounced out of her makeshift bun.

"Maybe we should workshop what *you* were up to last night?" Judith suggested.

"I reckon your need is greater than mine right now."

That, Judith reflected as she grabbed a cup of coffee from the self-serve espresso machine, was probably true.

"I've only got twenty minutes," Polly explained as Judith sat down opposite her. "I've got to run a counselling session."

Judith took a deep breath and launched in. "Carts came to dinner last night." Polly's eyebrows waggled in an I-thought-as-much gesture. "And I cooked this amazing meal from Ottolenghi."

"Who?"

"Never mind. And then we listened to music—did you know he's into collecting eighties LPs?"

"Yeah, it's been a thing of his ever since uni."

"Well, it was fun and we danced and he mimed his—"

"Mark Knopfler?"

"Oh yes! You've seen him do that?"

"Every karaoke evening since 2011."

Judith felt her insides melt. "That's so sweet. So anyway, then we danced, and um, one thing kind of led to another and…"

"You know I won't be shocked Jude. Just as few or as many details as you like."

"Well, he um, how can I put this?" Judith leaned over the table and hiss-whispered, "He did things to me, really lovely things…" Her hair fell over her shoulder and a strand nearly made it into her coffee. She moved the cup. "But he wouldn't let me do *anything* to him, past the kissing stage." She cast a swift glance at Polly, who was looking thought-ful. "I just wondered if that's—normal."

"Depends what you call normal."

"Oh, um—" Judith looped her hair behind both ears. Her earlobes were hot, which meant she must be blushing madly.

Polly clasped her hands together and leaned in too. "If you mean, is this what can happen to guys when they're anxious and maybe a bit out of practice, yes. Jude, it's not just us girls that have issues with the big O. Men do too. Much more than they let on."

"I guess so. I just don't have much recent experience to go by."

"It's not always a case of get hard, get thrusting, and *voila!*" Polly snapped her fingers. "Guys can get performance anxiety, particularly early on in a relationship. If things are a little hyperactive in that depart-ment, it's not that easy to admit."

Of course, it made total sense now Polly explained it like that. She'd been so worried about her own lack of experience, of putting him off by being too keen... and then last night, she was so overwhelmed by her own needs that she'd been blind to what could be going on for him.

"If that's it... what can I do? To help us get past it?" What if they never could? What if she never got to see Carts naked? To touch him, feel him deep inside her?

"You need to talk about it with him."

"But he hasn't said that's the problem. I can't assume—"

"Okay," Polly's face got into its professional groove. "Here's the plan. There's a book, it's called *Pleasure Your Partner*, by... some sex therapist," She snapped her fingers again. "Dianne—no, Daphne that's it, Dr Daphne Rubekind. Wow, I'm amazed I remember her name, it's a while since I needed that book, years actually." Judith grinned ruefully. Oh to be in Polly's shoes. "It's about how to enjoy the full experience of love-making, physically and psychologically."

"Can I download it onto my reading device?"

"I doubt it. It's probably out of print, it was written in the 1990s."

Judith's face fell, her hopes dashed. "Oh."

"But there's almost definitely a copy at the Book Genie. At least there was ten years ago!"

"Ten years ago!" Judith echoed in disbelief.

"Yeah." Polly mused. "I hid it in the Ancient History section."

Judith's eyes widened. "What did you do that for?"

Polly shrugged. "I used to read it when I worked there as a student. I'd shove it on the top shelf so no one would find it. Honestly, *nobody* went near that section—except a dear old retired professor who was always asking for books on Ancient Mesopotamia. But I reckon he's probably dead now. So, anyway, I'm pretty sure it'll be there."

Judith could only gape. "Wouldn't they have done a stocktake since then?"

"Rowena, do a stocktake? Are you joking? She just piles in more books. Anyway... It's a little red book, jam-packed with tips, it really opened my eyes."

The thought of Polly ever needing her eyes opened with regard to sex was kind of funny. But if this book delivered her an ounce of Polly's confidence in the bedroom, then she'd be happy. And if it helped her and Carts to... excitement fluttered inside her like a swarm of butterflies.

"Thank you Polly," she said gratefully. "So am I to assume that you and the owner of the leather jacket have a thing going?"

"Shitbags, look at the time." Polly jumped up and grabbed the jacket.

"That's not fair." Judith laughed. "I've laid bare all my intimate secrets; you can't walk out without—"

"I'll tell all later." Polly hugged the jacket to her chest and Judith could have sworn she bent her head and gave it a little sniff. "Go buy that book. It'll give you heaps of advice."

And then she left.

Honestly, thought Judith, watching Polly's departing figure, if that girl had a tail-feather she'd be shaking it right now.

"No lady friend tonight?" Paddy the Shamrock barman raised an eyebrow as Carts sat down at the bar.

"She's got a family commitment, otherwise she'd be here." He couldn't stomach the thought of looking like a loser, even to Paddy, who never judged. "Two of the usual. Dan'll be joining me."

"Righto." Paddy grinned.

To be brutally honest, an evening with Dan at the Shamrock wasn't going to measure up to making love to Judith tonight. But in the mix was a grain of relief. In all honesty, he wasn't ready to trust his body. Sure, Tantra had served him well last night, but really if it had come to Judith focusing on him, touching him, he could so easily have let himself down and put paid to his chances.

Here's a rose, now squeeze the base of my dick.

Carts stifled a grimace as he ordered two pints from Paddy.

He'd forced himself to attend a later session of yoga this evening. Decided to go to a Vinyassa class and pumped out warrior poses and sun salutes until he'd raised a sheen of sweat.

Despite having worked off a pile of energy, he was still wired. Too many images of Judith, the scent of her, the feel of her, the way she called his name as she came, running through his brain, making his libido difficult to keep under wraps.

A hard slam between the shoulder blades made him wince. He'd have to tell Dan to stop the fuck creeping up on him.

"Mate, you made it." Dan sounded astounded.

"Course I made it."

"I can't tell anymore with you," Dan grumbled, swinging his butt onto a bar stool. "You'll disappear up your own arse one day with all this hippy shit."

"Better than teabagging into the mouth of one of your team mates every Saturday arvo. It's surprising you don't talk like thiiiissss." Carts raised his voice to a shrill pitch.

"Cock sucker," Dan retorted cheerfully.

"Yeah, and that too." They both laughed. Puerile jokes had always been the order of Friday nights, a pint of the black stuff in front of you, possibly a line of them. It was a relief sometimes, the banter Carts only ever indulged in with his best mates; safe in the knowledge it would go no further.

Dan's freckles shone in the Shamrock lights. He really looked no different from when he was thirteen, just a bit taller and a hell of a lot broader.

Built like a brick shitter, I am, Dan had always said proudly.

They guzzled their pints in unison. Elbows bent, glasses to mouth. The great Guinness salute. The loud lip smack of satisfaction before licking away the froth moustache.

Back like it used to be. Minus one important cog in the wheel.

As if he read his mind, Dan said, "Have you heard from Aaron lately?"

Carts flicked a quick glance to see Dan's pale blue eyes suddenly examining the ceiling, the look he got when a) he was pissed as a fart or b) he was being evasive about something. He guessed Dan had got the big news too and he supposed he should help him out by letting him know he knew.

"Yeah, he rang to say him and Alice have got engaged."

"Oh, right-oh." Still Dan's gaze was evasive. "And… you're all cool with that?"

Carts grinned. "I told him no hard feelings as long as I'm still best man."

Dan looked relieved. "Bugger, I thought he'd choose me."

"No way he would, you'd drop the ring down a crack in the podium. Then get maggoted and upset the bridesmaids with your god-awful chat-up lines."

"Bullshit." But Dan had the grin of a man who knew, from experience, this to be the case. "Mind you," he added after another slug of his pint, "it did make me think if Aaron could find 'the one', there's hope."

"Hope for what?"

"The likes of you and me."

"Speak for yourself."

Dan plonked his empty glass on the bar. "Awright, but let's be honest, mate. Neither of us are exactly high on the pulling power, are we?"

Carts squared his shoulders, ruffled a hand through his hair. Fuck it, he was going to get that haircut tomorrow morning from Tara, walk into the jaws of terror and let her snip her worst.

"Speak for yourself," he muttered, rubbing the condensation from the sides of his glass.

Dan's eyes took on a gleam of interest. "About to plunge in again are you mate?" He sounded a little peeved, almost envious. Dan might eschew dating for rugby, but Carts knew behind that solid wall of muscle he was soft as butter. They'd never have maintained a friendship if he wasn't.

"You ever see Lucy these days?" Dan asked now.

"No way!" Carts shuddered. Lucy had lived with him for a few months, and he'd foolishly believed for a time she was "the one". He'd given himself over to her whims and fancies. Her insomnia and her constant worry about whether she should have Botox for a tiny invisible —to him—crease in the centre of her forehead that no-one would even notice, let alone care about. They'd been a disaster together sexually. He'd had completely the opposite problem with Lucy. Frankly, he'd barely dare get a half mongrel around her in case she complained about it prodding her in the back and keeping her awake.

He brought her breakfast.

Listened to her woes about her job.

Paid for twelve sessions with a personal trainer for her birthday.

Hadn't—as far as he was aware—paid for her to shag the personal trainer as part of the elite wellness package at Fitbods gym. Obviously he'd failed to read the small print properly.

What had he ever seen in her?

The potential for a life he'd always longed for, that's what. The house, the kids, the white picket fence. The Aussie dream of trundling around the aisles of Bunnings on a Saturday morning, rug rats in tow, choosing tiles for the kitchen and paint samples for the front door.

"Well, she's no loss. You're better off without her," Dan said after ordering another two pints from Paddy. "How say you about a night at the casino to celebrate Aaron and Alice deciding to tie the knot?"

"Not really in the mood mate, to be honest."

Dan's face fell for a moment, but not easily put off, he said, "Tomorrow night then."

"Can't, I'm on standby for Avery."

Dan pulled a face. "I'd say I'd come, but you know, classical music isn't exactly my thing."

"Nah." Carts shook his head, frowning. "It's not her music. She's going to a friend's birthday party, and it's one of those gigs that might turn feral. Mum doesn't really want her to go but I said I'd take her and pick her up." What he didn't mention was the little rendezvous he'd arranged with Judith after. Right now, he wanted to keep his fledgling love affair to himself. It all felt too fragile and precious to be picked apart by Dan's unsubtle rugby hands.

"Need a back-up?"

Carts shook his head. "No, mate. I'm good. Shouldn't think anything'll go wrong, just my paranoid brain overreacting."

"I'd like to come anyway. Don't see much of you these days."

He opened his mouth to refuse and then caught the almost wistful expression that accompanied Dan's words. Carts realised that Dan was probably missing Aaron too. And yeah, if he was honest, he'd not been the best of mates lately, more interested in doing yoga and having a quiet drink with Judith afterwards than spending time with his oldest pal.

He softened. "Okay. Aves likes you. Maybe she won't make a thing about being dragged away early if you're there too. How about we go for a bite to eat first?"

Dan's face noticeably brightened. "Yeah, let's grab a curry, we haven't had one for weeks."

Carts would have preferred something a little less spicy on the breath, but he wasn't going to let Dan down when he had that hopeful look on his dial. "You've got a deal."

Dan held up his fist. Carts bumped knuckles with him.

They picked up their fresh pints of Guinness in unison.

"To Aaron and Alice," Dan said.

Yep. He'd drink to that.

CHAPTER 14

$\mathcal{G}$lide Physiotherapy took up the ground floor of a trendy office block on the south side of the city, the floor to ceiling windows plastered with photos of toned legs in running shoes and the words, *Why Run when you can Glide?*

With a quick hi to the receptionist, Lou, who she knew from meeting Pip here numerous times, Judith took a seat and listened to her sister's voice reverberate through the thinly partitioned wall. "Come on now, yes, bend a bit more for me, that's it. Press against me, now pull back... Ah, good one. See? You've got more range of movement already."

Judith picked up a magazine called *Keto* and stared blindly at an article about how to get your own fat to eat itself, which incidentally was not a problem she suffered from; a bit more flesh over her bones would probably be good. She threw *Keto* back on the pile and picked up a parenting magazine; flicked through pictures of little round heads and chubby fingers, could almost smell their sweet newborn scent and wondered what babies with Carts would look like. No doubt she'd birth babies who shot off the charts for length.

Crazy. One mind-blowing orgasm and she was fantasising about having Carts' babies. Was that the purpose of orgasms? To bond you to one another with a flash as blinding as the Big Bang?

She couldn't stop daydreaming; more precisely, she was *consumed* with thoughts of him—and turned on to the point of having to spend much of the day with her thighs squeezed together.

But that aside, it was also swoony romantic. She'd sneaked to her bag and read the note that she'd hidden in her purse several times. The special rose was now carefully arranged with the others in her favourite vase.

As Pip walked out, Judith threw the magazine back on the pile and jumped up.

Pip looked radiant. Judith recognised it as the look of love, the look Carts had on his face when she caught him staring at her. Oh stop it! This was the moment she had to focus on Pip's momentous announcement, not turn into a bag of mushy peas.

"Okay," said Pip as she closed the door, "sit down and listen." Judith obligingly hooked her bottom onto the treatment table. "I've rehearsed this with Shaz, but she doesn't know our family, so she wasn't sure if it would work. I'm trying to memorise it because reading it would be shite, *obviously.*"

"Okay. Go ahead."

Pippa cleared her throat and squared her shoulders, her strong quads shaping her work slacks, and read from her scribbled handwritten lines. "Mum and Dad, I—we—Shaz and I, have an announcement to make." Foot shuffle. "Oh, forgot to include Kirsty and Luke. Okay, so take that as given." She cleared her throat. "Shaz and I are in love. We want you to know we are very happy—" she stopped, "—ecstatically happy maybe?"

Judith nodded. "That's good," she agreed, but all she could see was Mum's face freezing up. "Though do you think perhaps, I don't know, maybe just make it a bit less emotive. Mention Shaz is your partner first before you say the love word."

"No way. That makes us sound like a business arrangement. It's got to be super clear or Mum will pretend she hasn't heard me."

Pippa dipped her chin and read out more lines.

"That's lovely," Judith said when she'd finished. "But, um, do you think a restaurant is the best place to tell them?"

Pip threw her head back. "Urfff. can you stop seeing all the problems? Besides, Harry's isn't just any restaurant, it's special."

"Have you warned Shaz? About how Mum reacts sometimes?"

"Kind of." Pip's face turned mischievous. "Perhaps I should forget the speech, and we'll strip each other's kit off and make out on the lazy Susan." She grinned. "Can you imagine Mum's face?"

She sucked her cheeks in and went cross-eyed.

"I just meant—"

Pippa raised her arms. "I've just got to do this, Jude— I mean, Shaz's parents totally embraced our relationship from the get-go. Then there's Mum and Dad like two old neutered cats—"

"Pip!"

"Oh c'mon, they are, and I'm just—pissed off, at how useless they are. Mum particularly, and Dad just goes along with it. Growing up with that, I've realised how much it's stunted me, sexually, emotionally, everything..."

Me too, Judith thought quietly. But still, it was complicated. "Go easy on Mum." She gave Pippa a pleading look. "She can't help her upbringing."

Pippa flapped the piece of paper on the desk. "Give me a break. I can't make excuses for her the way you do. I'm nearly twenty-three and I've only just had the courage to admit I'm gay, even to you and you're the closest person to me in the world. Shaz told her parents when she was thirteen she was a lesbian. That's the level of trust they share."

"How long have you known?"

"Since I was fourteen and Trent Tucker kissed me, and I wanted to throw up."

"Oh, dear." Judith grinned. Trent had been the most sought-after boy in her sister's year. She knew because of all the fourteen-year-old girls texting him selfies of themselves with their school blouse tucked into their bra. Pippa's school had finally clamped down on it.

Pippa paused. "Remember Tilly?"

Judith cast her mind back. "The blonde girl in your gang?"

"Yeah, we hung out a bit, kissed and what-not."

Judith frowned. "But she dated Trent for ages didn't she?"

Pippa nodded. "Bi."

Judith rubbed her forehead and out came the words she'd vowed she wouldn't say. "I'm so sorry, Pip."

"For what?" Pippa, loading hand weights into a box, turned and looked at her in surprise.

"That you went through all this alone. I wish you'd felt comfortable telling me."

"I could *never* have told you earlier," Pip said, almost vehemently "No offence babe, but you and Mark were so hetero and so *itemised.*" The term made Judith feel like a product on the shelf of Woolworths. Couple past their use-by date. "Besides," Pippa continued, "I couldn't come to terms with it myself for years. I just knew girls did it for me, and boys didn't." She stuck her finger into her open mouth and mock gagged. "Penises! Ball sacks. Urk."

Judith bit down on her smile. She didn't share the repugnance. The chance to see a bit more of Carts in that department would be most welcome. "You can hear through the walls you know," she pointed out.

Pip's eyes widened for a moment then she shrugged. "Don't care." She turned towards reception and with a mock bow said, "Meet Pippa Mellors, lesbian and proud." She swivelled back to Judith. "Honestly Jude, I'm so happy, I honestly don't care who knows."

Tears pricked Judith's eyes suddenly. "You're amazing, Pip."

"Just comfortable in my own skin at last." Pip gave Judith her lopsided screw-ball grin, the one she always passed off a compliment with. "I approve, by the way."

"Of what?"

"Of that Carts guy. Apart from his dreadful yoga pants, I definitely approve."

Judith demurred. "We're not like you and Shaz, committed or anything." *More's the pity.*

"He digs you big time."

"You think?" She almost blushed at how very much he'd seemed to dig her last night.

"*Yeah!*" Pippa rolled her eyes as she bounced an exercise ball into a corner of the room. "Slavish adoration written all over his face."

"That could just be his yogic enlightened look."

Pippa guffawed. "It was coming from a place a lot lower than his spiritual centre, let me tell you. Okay—" She flexed her muscles, picked up her bag and flung an arm round Judith's shoulders. "Let's do this, sis."

They met Shaz in the carpark outside the restaurant and the two women clasped hands tightly and gazed resolutely into each other's eyes.

"Ready for this?" Pippa said, kissing Shaz on the lips.

"Sure am." Shaz turned and embraced Judith. "And thanks for supporting us."

Judith hugged her back so tightly words were not needed.

"C'mon." Pippa had her pre-match face on, her mouth tight at the corners and her eyes scrunched as, hand in hand, the two women marched towards the neon sign marked "Harry Tan's".

Watching them, Judith choked up and could only smile out of teary eyes. Whatever happened tonight, she felt honoured to be here supporting Pippa and Shaz in their journey together.

Harry spotted them immediately as they walked in, and hurried forward. Of course Pippa had chosen Harry's restaurant. It was something of an icon in the gay and multicultural community of Perth. With his partner, Kun, Harry had perfected the best barbecued duck in the Southern Hemisphere. You couldn't visit Perth without being directed to the glossy red barbecued ducks hanging from the rotisserie in the window. The long lines outside the restaurant testified to its popularity —people happily queued for the privilege of eating here. Unless of course you'd built Harry and Kun's stunning home on the river. For that reason, John Mellors' family always had the private room at their disposal.

Mum and Dad and Luke and Kirsty were seated around a table piled with plates of money bags and crunchy spring rolls, and Dad had already tucked in.

Mum was smiling at Kirsty, who could be heard even before you entered the room. Kirsty was the face for Mellors Homes. She'd been a morning radio presenter before she married Luke, and always sounded like she was cheer-squadding a bleary-eyed 5 am audience.

Nowadays Kirsty's smile flashed from billboards around the city, in front of a Mellors home, with the words "Let OUR family build YOUR family's dream home" floating on puffy white clouds above her head.

"Hi there." Kirsty jumped up as if they had indeed come to view a display home.

Pip gave her a hug, high-fived Luke then went over to Mum, who didn't stand up but proffered her cheek. Pippa barely pecked it. Dad scraped his chair back and stood up, rubbing at his mouth with a napkin and gave Pip a quick squeeze. Judith followed suit and did the rounds.

Shaz had turned deathly pale as the introductions rolled on, as if the reality of the situation had finally hit her.

After everyone was seated and platefuls of glistening sliced duck and pancakes and bright green bok choy had been brought out, Dad said, "So Pip. What's the big announcement? We've all been betting on Andrew giving you a promotion?"

"Better actually." Pippa threw a look at Shaz. Scraping back her chair, she stood and steadied herself with hands splayed on the table and her biceps rigid.

"Mum, Dad. Luke and Kirsty—and Jude, well, you already know, don't you babe." She gave a big toothy nervous grin that made her look fourteen again. "I have an announcement to make." She grabbed Shaz's hand. "Shaz and I, that is, Shaz and me," an uncharacteristic little giggle followed, "are in love." Silence. Pippa's voice got louder. "She's the most important woman in the world to me and we're very happy. We wanted to be clear about our relationship from the start so that you can welcome her into the family, as my girlfriend."

No-one said a word. Somewhere out front, Kun could be heard calling, "Takeaway half duck for Colin." Judith sneaked a look from behind her hair. Kirsty had her mega-watt smile locked in place, Luke looked bemused, Dad rubbed vigorously at his mouth with his napkin and Mum stared at the tablecloth.

Oh Mum, please, please—just this once, Judith begged silently. *Override the fear and guilt that strangles the life out of you. Escape from the shadow of your past. Be bigger than that. Show Pippa that you love her, unconditionally.*

She had to sit on her hands and pin her lips together to stop herself from jumping up and saying something to fill the silence.

The next moment it was as if Dad took hold of himself from the inside out. And to give him his due, once he'd wiped the look of surprise off his face with that napkin it was clear he wasn't going to let his youngest daughter down.

"Well, that's big news Pip, er—nice to meet you Shaz. Does that stand for Sharon? Or should we all call you Shaz?"

Shaz's mouth broke into a relieved smile. "Shaz is fine."

"Well, Shaz, welcome to the family."

Another awkward silence, while Harry fussed around refilling their glasses. Kirsty suddenly gushed out "cool" and "wonderful" and Luke mumbled something that sounded affirmative.

Finally, Mum got to her feet and said to the tablecloth, "Will you excuse me while I go to the ladies' room?"

The rest of the meal passed in the awkward way events do when a great big elephant has landed in the middle of the table next to the Peking duck and everyone is studiously ignoring it.

It wasn't that Mum didn't talk to Shaz. She did. She was pleasant and polite. But it was as if Pippa had never spoken those words.

As the meal progressed, Judith could sense Pippa's energy building next to her like a brewing storm. Finally Pip jumped to her feet. "Mum," she said loudly, "are you going to acknowledge what I said?" Luke gave a nervous cough into the void.

Pippa sucked in a big breath. "You've never accepted my reality, have you? Ever since I was little and you made me wear those frilly-topped socks and horrible patent shoes."

Mum shook her head and stared blankly at a spot on the wall past Pippa's head.

Pip dodged her head into Mum's line of vision. Mum's gaze shifted three millimetres. "Mum! I'm gay. G.A.Y. I'm a lesbian. Do you understand what that *means*? It means I dig women."

Shaz put her hand on Pippa's arm and made a gentle shushing sound. But Pip wasn't going to be silenced. "I love Shaz, Shaz loves me. It's not the work of the devil. It's just another colour in the rainbow."

Mum made a strangled little sound and her hand fluttered to her neck. "You need to get your head around who I really am, see *me*, not some imaginary person you wish I was. I can't live like that, Mum, because that would mean living a lie and I won't do that to myself anymore. You have to accept me as I am..." She paused, her hands fisting at her sides, "because if you don't, I really can't—" her voice cracked. "I really can't see you anymore."

And with that she grabbed Shaz's hand, who hurriedly thanked them for the meal, and the two of them were gone.

The silence was filled with the chatter and laughter of happy diners on the other side of the glass partition.

A universe away from the Mellors family drama.

Judith got up, gagged out, "Excuse me a minute," and raced after the two women.

In the street she caught up with them. Grabbing Pip's arm, she swung her around. "Are you okay?"

"I'm fine," Pip said, her chest rising and falling rapidly. "It's Mum that's got the problem."

Judith stared into Pippa's eyes; they were hard and determined as steel. And then Pip shook her head. "I'm really sorry, I know I always leave you to deal with her, but I just can't cope with Mum's miserable, repressed view of the world anymore." They stood staring at each other, both silently acknowledging the inevitable.

Finally, Judith said softly, "You two go. I'll handle Mum."

As she headed back into Harry's she realised this was how it had always been.

Stuck in the middle between Mum and Pippa.

Desperately gluing the broken pieces back together and plastering over the cracks in between.

CHAPTER 15

Saturday

"*H*arder? Softer?"

Carts lay back, eyes closed, and let the bliss wash over him. "It's perfect, thanks."

Tara's fingertips continued to massage his scalp with the pressure only a true pro could exert. His whole body felt like a giant floating marshmallow as the massage chair sent ripples into the small of his back and his shoulders. Why had he been so worried about coming here? To think he'd put up with years of Bernie scrubbing his scalp raw, followed by a towel-dry that was more suited to a doggy wash than a hair salon.

Right now, he'd happily pay Tara for another half hour of this.

After she'd rinsed out the peppermint-scented conditioner and wrapped a towel round his hair and dried it with the gentleness a mother might administer to her favourite child, he found himself staring at his reflection in the mirror, and all the anxiety about having his hair cut evaporated.

He'd woken with a mild hangover from his Friday evening out with

Dan, and a determination to do the deed. This was no longer acceptable, he decided as he combed a long lock of hair one way and then the other, only for it to flop right back over his eyes.

So he'd made a list. Get a haircut. Purchase a new bottle of Eau d'homme. Buy a packet of…? His pen hovered over the letters, unable to complete the word "condoms". He hadn't needed them for a year and now he felt like he was being presumptuous, but… well, after Thursday… they were on the brink of something and he had to hope that Fern's teachings would work magic—

Tara, who'd disappeared to answer the phone, now returned with a little trolley full of exotic-looking implements. She took out some scissors with strangely scalloped edges to them and a comb.

"So what are we doing today?"

At which Carts launched into a lengthy description of how his hair behaved if it was cut wrongly. "So," he finished when he realised her nodding had increased to the point where it was clear she wanted him shut up, "that's my hair woes in a nutshell."

"Just a bit of shape around the front and ears then. A touch off the back so it doesn't flick up on your shirt collar."

He looked at Tara's refection in awe. "You reckon you could do that? Keep some length but get the shape back into it?"

"Hey," Tara pointed the scissors at her chest, where today the words, *Great hair doesn't happen by chance* were emblazoned in gold letters on a black background. "Trust me, sweetheart, okay?"

JUDITH HAD BARELY SLEPT. Images of the disastrous evening at Harry Tan's had churned through her head, invading her dreams and tying her into knots in her bed clothes.

When she'd arrived back at the restaurant, Dad had been paying the bill. He carried Mum's coat and ushered her through the door, mouthing to the others over her head, "Your mum just needs time to process." And then they were gone, leaving Judith and Luke and Kirsty standing on the pavement.

Kirsty said, "I guess we should have *suspected*," in the slightly incredulous tone of someone who inhabited a world of heterosexual couples with 2.2 kids. Luke cleared his throat. "That would account for why Pip never brought a boyfriend home." His troubled gaze fixed on her. "You'll talk to Mum won't you Jude?" he said. "Get those two back on track."

Judith stared at her parents' departing figures. Dad, bulky shouldered and protective; Mum bent as if pushing against the wind, even though the air was perfectly still.

"I don't know if I can anymore," she'd said and swallowed the lump forming in her throat.

Sitting up in bed now, she decided affirmative action was needed. Not the kind of action that meant fixing other people's lives. She'd done too much of that over the years, today she had her own to fix. With sudden determination, she got up, showered, dressed and, after a piece of toast and marmalade and a coffee, made her way into the city.

When she arrived at the Book Genie she browsed the shelves of mystery books outside, all packaged in brown paper with clues hand-written on labels. She wondered if Alice had written them, because she only managed to guess one, the hints were so clever and obscure. Eventually, she plucked up her courage and sidled through the doors and along the aisles of floor-to-ceiling bookshelves, until she reached the Ancient History section. The yellowing sign hung off its nail, the letters fading and the cardboard curled at the edges.

She scanned the top shelf and her heart dropped. No little red volume as far as she could see. She squinted—this part of the shop was dimly lit—and then she spied it, squeezed in, right at the end of the shelf, like an afterthought. A bright red spine in all the dull scholarly titles. For once, she was thankful to be over six foot. Standing on tiptoes, her fingers scrabbled to reach it. She managed to tug it from the shelf, catching it just before it hit her in the eye.

There was one embossed rose on the cover, which struck her as a good omen. She flipped it open and read the title page:

Pleasure Your Partner
A manual for lifelong loving

By Dr Daphne Rubekind

Sneaking the book behind her handbag, Judith went to find somewhere to sit. The wonderful thing about the Book Genie was that there were reading seats in every nook and cranny; stools shaped like toadstools and frogs in the children's section, a big Alice in Wonderland throne at the end of the Fantasy section, and square trompe l'oeil cubes painted to look like shelves of books. She perched on one of them in a quiet corner and eagerly turned the pages.

The first gem she came to was "Take Your Time". She guessed that's where she'd gone wrong, jumped in too fast and eager with the hip grind move down by the river when they'd kissed. She'd more or less rubbed herself all over him like marinade and from what Polly said, that could have been somewhat overwhelming.

She flicked eagerly through more pages and found a chapter on touch. Her eyes widened as she read through all the tips and little tricks. Tongues, lips, thighs, breasts, you name it; there was not one piece of your anatomy you couldn't put to good use.

But it was the chapter on Barriers to Intimacy that resonated the most. Dr Rubekind had a lot to say on good old-fashioned talking things through. It was all very sound advice. She skimmed to the end of the chapter where a little shaded box summarised the main points.

REMEMBER: Great sex involves the brain far more than the reproductive organs. Many barriers to sexual intimacy are psychological, not physical. Talk about your likes and dislikes, deepest desires and greatest fears with your partner. A truly wonderful physical connection develops when you can be open and honest with one another.

"THANK YOU, *thank you*, Dr Daphne Rubekind," Judith whispered, clasping the little volume to her chest. Because now she knew that there really was nothing to worry about. Sure, there were some hurdles to overcome, but there was nothing *wrong* with either of them. They loved each other's company, they made each other laugh and their chemistry was off the charts. The rest would follow once they relaxed and learned to open up and... just *talk* to one another.

Holding the book like a precious artefact she'd uncovered in an archaeological dig, Judith made her way to the counter, and didn't even blink when the woman flipped it open, revealing the title in big bold letters.

"I can't find a price anywhere," the woman said finally. "How about I charge you ten dollars?"

"Ten dollars is absolutely fine." Judith smiled sweetly and got out her purse.

CHAPTER 16

"When you turn the corner, stop the car."

Avery had jumped into the passenger seat with her duffle coat bundled around her and a bulky plastic bag clasped to her chest.

"What for?" Carts tried to keep his voice neutral because the teenage energy next to him was at risk of setting fire to the car.

"You don't think I'm going like this, do you?" Avery cast an urgent glance at the house and hissed, "Quick, drive off before Mum comes out to check what I'm wearing."

Shaking his head, Carts pushed the gear stick into drive and drove off down the street. Only when they'd turned the corner did Avery slump back against the seat with a sigh of relief. Then she started to tug things out of the bag; a pair of high-heeled sparkling silver sandals, a compact of eye shadows the size of a paintbox, a pair of dangly diamanté earrings and a bottle of Passion Pop.

"You're not taking alcohol." Carts almost exploded.

"It's not for me. It's for the others." Hastily, she shoved the bottle back into the bag.

"But you're all underage."

"No, Duke's nineteen."

"I told you I don't want you being around that guy."

Avery clucked her tongue loudly. "I can't just ignore him if he speaks to me, can I?"

"You can walk away."

"Thatsadumbasfuckidea." Avery had by now yanked down the passenger seat mirror and was popping her eyes at her reflection and puffing her lips into a pout.

"Can you pleassse stop the car," she whined. "I can't put my make-up on while you're driving."

"Only if you promise you won't drink that shit."

"Argggh, okay, promise."

Exasperation rising up his throat like acid, Carts veered to the side of the road and drew to a halt with a squeal of brakes. Apart from when he drove into Ron's parking spot, he was a meticulously careful driver but right now, his last surviving nerve was hanging on by a thread.

Why did he sense the evening was going to go downhill from here? He tried to push the thought away, tried to be positive. Because if everything went to plan he'd be seeing Judith at the end of the night, maybe even... he made an effort to tone down the adrenaline that had his heart drumming against his ribs.

"You'd better mean that." He focused on sounding stern, only to relent as Avery nuzzled his arm with her chin. "You're the best," she replied before resuming her make-up.

He sat watching her out the corner of his eye and pretended to check his phone.

A brush that would have done Picasso proud swept over her cheekbones. Lipstick was applied, and then she brought out some things that looked like two furry caterpillars.

"What the fuck?" he said, unable not to stare, as she carefully fixed them to her upper eyelids.

"Magnetic eyelashes," she said proudly. "I mean, *how cool* are these?"

"Christ!"

After a few more moments of admiring her reflection, Avery shoved the passenger door open and stepped out of the car.

"Where are you going?" He leaned over the seat only to see her wriggle out of her thick duffle coat, fluff out her hair and, hopping on one leg, she grabbed a shoe from the floor of the car, shoved it onto her foot and then did the same with the other. It was like watching a moth emerge from a chrysalis. She bent down and stared in at him and he had to avert his eyes from her pushed up breasts. She was his little sister, he didn't need to see she was growing into a woman.

Carts barely recognised the face in front of him.

Cute, wide-eyed Avery had turned into a smoky-eyed beauty.

Somewhere in those features he caught a shadow of the kid she'd been only ten minutes before. Horror mixed in equal measure with admiration. Because she looked amazing. But it was like she'd thrown on a magic cloak, and she had no idea of its power.

Especially when her typical little Avery voice demanded, "Whatdyathink?"

His mouth drew tight as he struggled for words.

Crimson lips quivered, and her eyes squeezed as she wailed, "You don't think I look pretty."

Any minute now she was going to slam the car door and teeter off into the night. He couldn't let that happen.

"You look beautiful, Aves, I'm not used to it, that's all." He put his hand out in a placatory gesture. "Now get back in the car and tell me where Zammy lives."

They drove the rest of the way in silence, and the churning in his stomach didn't relent when they drew up outside a house throbbing with the heavy beat of music and the silhouettes of bodies gyrating at every window.

It felt like he was throwing Avery to the wolves. Avery, on the contrary, looked like she used to when she was about to dive into the coloured balls at IKEA. Even a thick coat of make-up couldn't cover that level of glee.

She shot out the car, grasping her little purse and her bottle of Passion Pop, dived back in to kiss him on the cheek and giggled, "Don't let your new girlfriend see that lipstick mark on your cheek. Thanks, goofballs, loveyaforever."

"Be ready at ten sharp, okay?" he called out, but she simply tossed her head and slammed the door. With a heavy heart he watched her slender legs on the cusp between child and woman as she wobbled up the path, her bare shoulder blades sticking out like wing buds above that tiny scrap of dress.

He shouldn't let her go in there.

But how the hell could he stop her now?

~

JUDITH THREADED her sewing machine and found her favourite podcast, *The Very Serious Crafts* on her phone apps. Another quick glance at the clock showed it wasn't even 9 pm. The time had been dragging like the minute hand had weights attached to it. In her head she ran through the details again. Carts had said he'd pick up Avery at 10 sharp. By the time he'd taken her home it would be 10.30 and he'd be round at hers by 10.45 the latest. How could that still be so far away?

She'd spent the afternoon making pots of tea, reading *Pleasure Your Partner* (she'd found some very innovative techniques, along with Dr Rubekind's gems of wisdom about communication).

She was so excited to start this phase of her journey with Carts.

Resolutely, Judith tapped her screen and the podcast started up. She got the thread to go through the needle of her sewing machine, and with her foot controlling the pedal, fed the material of the blouse she was making through it.

As always, when she got going on anything crafty, time looked after itself.

Which was why the next thing she knew, the podcast was over and both sleeves were sewn into place. She turned the blouse the right way round and held it up. It was Liberty print material, which was often hard to find, a symphony of tiny flowers, the material the kind of soft cotton that felt lovely against your skin. She'd bought a couple of metres a year or so back in a sale when she'd been on holiday in Melbourne. Surveying her handiwork, she noticed she'd puckered the stitches around the placement of the right sleeve. Damn it, she mustn't have been concentrating. With a frustrated huff, she'd started to unpick the stitches when the doorbell rang.

Her nerves lit up.

Surely not Carts already? She hadn't even got changed. Oh lord, she was sitting here in her bra, sewing. Unable to locate the T-shirt she'd just removed, she hurriedly put on the blouse instead. Heart thumping madly, she ran to the door and flung it open, only to have her mouth fall open in horror.

Mark was standing on the doorstep.

"Hi." He grinned.

'Oh—hi?"

They stared at each other.

"Are you going to leave me standing out here in the cold?"

"It's not cold," she pointed out.

"Well—anyway, can I come in?"

Before she could even think of refusing, he'd strolled past her, down the passage and into the kitchen with the air of someone who still lived here.

Judith scurried after him. "Are you looking for something? I'm pretty sure I brought the rest of your stuff over the other day."

"No, no. Though I could do with a brownie."

"I don't have any."

"Seriously? Anyway, I've got some news." He popped his eyes and lifted his eyebrows. "We've *advanced*."

What was he talking about? She must have stared blankly because he said with slight exasperation, "To the next level. We've decided we need to take our proposal to GameX."

She rubbed at the line between her eyebrows. "Sorry, what?"

"Smidge." Mark's lower lip protruded. "I know you were never that interested in what I do. But come on, GameX is the biggest gaming convention in the world."

"Oh, right."

"Which means…" His look turned suddenly shifty. "I need to borrow a bit more cash. I'll pay you back with interest once it's been accepted. Which is a dead cert, of course. We're going to make squillions."

Something inside her threatened to snap. "You stole my savings, and now you're asking for more."

He planted his feet wide. "They were *our* savings. And I didn't steal. I borrowed. And only because I had to spend my share on the bond and rent. That wasn't really fair."

"You chose to leave." She stifled a little shudder. Thank heavens he had.

He waggled his brows. "Maybe we could rethink that. After GameX."

"What?" Her eyes widened in horror. "No!"

"Oh c'mon, Smidge." He put on his puppy dog look. Ew, how could she ever have found it remotely cute? "We were okay together."

"Maybe once, years ago. When we'd actually do things together. You didn't even want to be with me on holiday, remember?"

"I did, just not Scotland. We went to Japan two years ago. That was good."

"Yes, because it coincided with a gaming convention." She flicked a glance at the clock. Suddenly it seemed time had decided to speed up. "This discussion is going nowhere, you should lea—"

"I was thinking if you gave me a loan for another three grand, that's tidy isn't it? And I'll pay you back all of it after we've got the contract signed."

Her mouth gaped. "You're crazy." Now the tightness had spread to her scalp. "Besides, I don't have it."

"Yeah, you do."

"I don't."

"How about your dad? He'd give you a loan if you asked. He's loaded."

"No WAY!"

He looked incredulous. "You have no idea how big this is going to be."

"No, Mark. I'm not asking Dad. I'm not enabling you anymore."

He gave a scoff. "Don't use your snotty therapy words on me."

Judith summoned every bit of strength she had. "I want you to leave. Get out of my house and go. And I want my money back. All of it."

He stared at her armpit and she realised the stitches she'd unpicked had left a gaping hole. "I always supported your crafting shit, why can't you support my interests?"

His barefaced lie almost winded her. She'd retreated into craft because all the intimacy with him had gone.

She stood up and drew her shoulders back.

"Do you know what I've learnt since you left, Mark? Relationships need work from both partners. Give and take." Seriously murderous thoughts ran through her head. "And frankly, all you've done these past few years is take."

Mark gave her a hurt look. The minute hand of the clock above his head shifted to 10.36.

Now, as well as wanting to strangle him, Judith was beginning to panic.

MEETING DAN for a curry had been a mistake. Like, seriously, what a dumb as shite idea to eat curry before a night with the woman of your dreams. Okay, the plan was he'd avoid his favourite garlic naan, stick to plain rice and something really mild in the spice department.

"How about we order a chicken phall?" Dan said as they walked into the plush deep red and gold interior of Vavoom Vindaloo. "Give ourselves the ultimate challenge?"

Carts shook his head. "You go for it, I'll stick with veggo tonight."

"No way, dude. You're turning into a fucking rabbit. I'll have to sever ties if you go on like this." He punched Carts' arm playfully. They both knew they'd still be mates in the nursing home, probably trundling down on their gophers to Vavoom Vindaloo if it still existed.

"You have a phall, and blow your sphincter out. Self-torture's lost its appeal lately," Carts said. After they'd been shown to their table, he perused the menu desperately. Maybe he'd settle for the kids' nuggets and chips.

A vegetable biryani was probably the safest bet.

When their dishes arrived, Dan rubbed his hands together. "Watch me clean this up."

"And wait for it to clean *you* out." Carts couldn't help a smirk. "Hope you've got nothing planned for tomorrow morning, mate."

"Just a date with the dunny." Dan sniggered and started to shove forkfuls of red sauce-covered chicken into his mouth. Carts snapped off a bit of pappadum and looked askance from under his newly trimmed fringe. Dan would need to clean up his act—literally—if he ever wanted a relationship that lasted longer than a weekend.

He wondered how his own dating position would be by tomorrow morning. It felt like he was about to walk across broken glass or hot coals, or possibly both. He could see some wonderful place on the other side, but the anticipation was pure torture.

His throat closed up and he nearly choked on a morsel of pappadum. Was he ready to take the next step?

It had been amazing giving Judith pleasure, but he knew she wanted to return the favour. And heck, he wanted that too. Desperately.

But he'd only attended one Tantra session. Learning this stuff was a lifetime's work. Who was he kidding here, thinking that because he'd managed to curb his desire and bring Judith to a screaming climax once, that would suffice?

Okay—Maybe they could just lie on the bed and cuddle and he'd pluck up the courage to tell her about his little problem. Nope, back up the truck. That was not going to happen.

Jesus Christ, he was more anxious than he'd ever been dating a woman before.

And then it struck him. Sure, he could give, but could he take? Could he open his heart and relax into the possibility that Judith could truly care about him?

Could he open up and simply trust?

All this nibbled at the back of his mind like a manic squirrel while he crunched through pappadums and ate his biryani, which seemed innocuous enough, and a bowl of salad. He had breath freshener along with the pack of condoms in the car. He'd also packed a toothbrush and he was wearing silk boxers, which kept rubbing disconcertingly and sending frissons of sensation to his groin.

He tried to focus on Dan, who was talking about choosing the new captain of his rugby team.

"Go on, dare you to try some," Dan said, gesturing with his fork. A bead of sweat trickled down his cheek and his eyes were watering profusely.

Carts shook his head. Not a hope in hell of him risking any other disasters below the waist. His dick was enough to contend with.

He'd just decided he'd eaten enough—his anxiety had made his stomach feel like a tightly closed fist anyway—when a vibration from his phone on the table drew his gaze. Then another.

He pulled it over with a frown, and the knot in his stomach intensified. Don't let this be Judith cancelling. Shit, why did his mind always have to go there?

Alarm bells rang as he realised it was Avery. Even his cracked phone screen couldn't hide the message behind the words.

Come and get me.

Now!

He jumped up, knocking the table so that Dan's fork jabbed into the side of his mouth, which gave rise to a loud exclamation along the lines of "clumsy fucker".

He didn't care. "Come on, we've got to go," he said as he thumbed into his screen *on my way.*

"What's happened?"

"Avery's in some kind of trouble."

"Was that who the message was from?"

"Yeah."

"Maybe she's just bored."

"That's not how it came over. Come on."

Still chewing and sweating, Dan stood and felt around in his back pocket for his wallet. "I'll get this one, you barely ate anything anyway."

"Thanks," Carts said, speeding for the door.

By the time Dan joined him he already had the engine revving and they took off into the busy Saturday evening traffic.

When they drew up outside the party house, the heavy beat of music could be heard even before he killed the engine. As they took the path up to the house, it was clear things were getting messy. There were kids milling all over the front patio and lawn, shouting and squealing with laughter. A girl was holding her friend's hair away from her face while she vomited into a bush; a couple were making out by the front door. Carts averted his eyes.

Inside, they got a few weird looks as they shouldered their way along the packed hallway.

When they reached the kitchen, Carts anxiously skimmed the heads, looking for Avery's chestnut brown hair. Knowing that she'd be a good head taller than most of the other kids here, panic set in when he couldn't see her. He was getting more strange looks; he understood why. Him and Dan were clearly the odd ones out; too young to be a parent and too old to be one of them. The crowd moved like parting waves to let him and Dan pass, eyeing them over the rims of their glasses with the hazy bloodshot look that came with too much alcohol consumption and dope.

Fuck! Where *was* Avery?

And then he spotted a glint of purple hair. Big hoop earrings, dark-rimmed eyes. Zammy, leaning against the kitchen sink, smoking a giant riff. Holding it between two purple-tipped fingers, she puffed smoke from out of her lower lip and didn't look surprised or even interested when her eyes met his.

He pushed through the throng towards her.

"Your Ave's brother aren't you?" She took a sip of red wine out of a plastic cup.

"Yes, she messaged me fifteen minutes ago. Do you know where she is?"

Zammy shrugged. "No idea." She called out, "Hey, Brett, have you seen Aves?"

A hairy guy slouched over. "Last I saw of her she was with Duke. But that was half an hour ago."

A ball of fire took over Carts' chest.

Vocal cords quivering with rage, he gritted out, "You better get your arse into gear, RIGHT NOW and help me find her."

~

HUGE TERRIFIED EYES. That's all he registered when the door to the bathroom flew open with the full force of Dan's shoulder behind it.

Adrenaline did the rest. In two strides Carts was pulling the guy off her, spinning him round by his collar.

"Fuckin' hell—" Duke's eyes were bloodshot, the words slurred. And then something that resembled a human bullet catapulted past Carts' left elbow. It took a moment to register that Dan now had Duke pinned up against the bathroom tiles, his feet dangling three centimetres off the floor.

"You little piece of shit." Dan's fists were white-knuckled as he gripped Duke by the front of his T-shirt, his jaw jutting as he eyeballed him. "What were you doing to her?"

"Get off me, you fucked up weirdo." Duke's legs were wheeling in the air. Meanwhile, in two strides Carts made it to where Avery was cowering next to the toilet. "Are you okay?" She nodded mutely, pulling her skirt down over her thighs with trembling fingers. He ripped off his jacket and put it round her shoulders, helped her to her feet, barely daring to think what would have happened if he hadn't seen her message.

"You're the fucked-up weirdo, mate." Dan was shouting now, his nose an inch from Duke's. "You're lucky I don't ram those teeth down your ugly throat."

"Stop it!" Avery's face was sheet white. "Please stop; can we just leave?"

"He hasn't hurt you, has he?" Carts asked quietly. She shook her head, even as her lower lip trembled and her eyes welled. "I'm okay, it didn't get that far."

Slightly reassured, Carts took hold of Dan's arm firmly. "Let him go, mate."

He felt Dan resist, then he gave Duke a final shake for good measure and dropped him.

"Piece of shit," he muttered, dusting off his palms.

In his moment of reprieve, Duke made a beeline for the door. Carts immediately stepped across the doorway, staring him down.

"Duke," he said with icy calmness, "you need to apologise to my sister."

As if his name pulled him up short, Duke's gaze skittered to Carts' face, then away. "I didn't do anything she didn't want," he muttered.

The icy control inside Carts threatened to turn into blistering rage. "You know that, eh? You know that for a fact, do you Duke?"

Duke was worrying at his lower lip with his teeth and swaying slightly, still pissed, but sobering up by the minute. Carts' eyes never left his face. "Did you ask, 'Is this what you want, Avery? Do you like the way I'm touching you, or would you rather I took my hands off your body?'" He bit back the bile rising in his throat. "Do you understand the word no, Duke?"

"She never said no—"

Now it was his turn to want to pin the guy up against the wall, but before he could do anything he might regret, Avery stepped forward. "I did say no," she said hotly. "I said I wasn't happy being in here with you alone. I said could we go back to the party…"

"What bit of that didn't you get?" Dan growled, rolling up his sleeve, ready to go back in for another round of pin the arsehole to the wall.

Carts stuck his arm out again, this time to stop Dan, and drew himself up to his full six foot six and a half.

"Apologise to my sister."

Silence.

"I said, apologise. Because you sure as hell aren't leaving this room until you do. And you'd better fucking mean it."

Now there was only the rasp of their adrenaline-fuelled breath. "Sorry," Duke finally muttered to the floor.

"Look her in the eyes when you speak."

"Aw fuck, will you let up? Okay, sorry." Duke glanced at Avery then away. "I thought you were into it too."

Carts' feet had never felt so firmly planted. Power flowed into his chest and shoulders. Next to him, he felt Avery's indignation flare as she too drew back her shoulders. "And I thought you were a nice person." She kicked off her shoes and stood proud in her natural glorious height. "I thought you liked me, for me. But you aren't nice. You're horrible and this is a horrible party and you're all—" she bent down, picked up one shoe and hurled it at his shin, "—horrible." Ignoring Duke's yelp of pain, she curled her hand into Carts' and with her head held high said, "Please take me home."

For the most part they drove in silence. Avery snuffled and Carts kept a hand over hers whenever he didn't need it for steering.

They dropped Dan off on the way, since his apartment was en route. Dan reached over the back seat and rubbed Avery's shoulder. "You alright, Aves?" She nodded. "Despite tonight, not all guys are complete arseholes."

"I know." She dimpled under her hair and Carts' shoulders relaxed a tad to see her cheeky spirit returning. "Just most of them."

"You got your own back with your stiletto," Dan said.

"Yeah, I reckon."

"I could go back and get them for you."

"They were ten dollars at Best and Less. And I couldn't walk in them anyway."

"Made good missiles, though. Nice shot." Next, Dan pushed a gentle fist into Carts' shoulder. "You did good tonight. I'd probably have been arrested for assault, but you gave it to him just with the verbals. Man, I admire that."

He gave Carts a headlock hug over the back of the seat then shifted his butt out and slammed the door. "Talk soon," he said with a wave, and Carts watched his friend's powerful frame pound up the path and take the stairs to his apartment.

When they got home, he pulled the plastic bag out from under the seat where Avery had lodged it. Had that really been a mere three hours ago? He felt suddenly weary, like the lifeblood had been drained out of him. "Do you want to put your coat on?"

Avery shrugged. "Nah. Doesn't matter if Mum sees me like this. It's going in the bin anyway. Stupid dress."

Carts smiled into the darkness as he cut the ignition.

"Okay, c'mon then. Let's face the music," he said.

"That's not actually funny right now."

As it happened, there *was* music playing as they went up the drive. Avery's face lit up. "Mozart's Concerto for Flute and Harp, second movement." She stopped, head tilted, listening. "Wait, the flute joins the harp... now." She beamed at him as, sure enough, the dulcet duet of harp and flute floated down the garden path from the house.

"It's my very favourite piece to play," she said.

He put his arm around her and she rested her head against his shoulder as they continued walking.

"I've neglected my music so much. And my friends at orchestra. I've been so mean to Bec, the lead violinist. I feel so bad."

"Don't." He stroked her hair off her forehead. "It's a valuable life lesson in what really matters. And better to learn it now, huh?"

"Mmm, guess so." She snuggled into him and he saw the goosebumps stand out on her arm under the porch light.

When Mum threw the door open her jaw dropped as she surveyed Avery in her little morsel of silver.

"Good lord Avery, you didn't wear that did you?"

"Shhhhh." Carts put his finger to his lips and escorted his sister inside. "She's had a rough time."

"Well, I'm not surpri—"

He shook his head and a little hiccup came from Avery.

"Not now Mum," he said. "Just be kind."

His mum's face crumpled as she looked from him to her daughter. Avery stood with her hands dangling and her head low. And then he knew Mum got it; without the need for words, she knew exactly what to do. "Oh, darling..." Her voice cracked with emotion as she held her arms wide.

With a sob, Avery walked straight into them.

"Are you sure there's no brownies in here?"

Judith dug her nails into her palm as Mark strolled over to the pantry and opened it.

"I haven't felt the need to make any recently." Mark either didn't notice the bitter edge to her voice or chose to ignore it. If this fiasco went on much longer, she'd have to push him physically out the front door. "Could you go now, please?" she said for what felt like the hundredth time.

His eyes rounded. "Why so snarky? Are you about to get your period?"

It took everything she had not to fly at his throat. But if she escalated this, he'd stay longer just to play smartarse, to try and wear her down. "I'm really tired, that's all."

She watched with distaste as he foraged in the cupboard, a sliver of flabby flesh showing around the waist of his jeans as he reached up, found the biscuit jar, took off the lid and peered inside. "Shortbreads. Better than nothing." He put the jar on the bench, removed one and munched. "I'll tell you what, I'll email you our business plan. Under peril of death, do NOT show it to anyone. You'll change your mind when you see what we've put together. It's going to be huge. You'll get your six grand back ten times over. It's called MegaV, Wars Within the Multi-verse." He rattled off some more jargon and now the clock above his head said 10.46 and she just had to get him out of here.

"Okay," she said, jumping off her stool. "Email me whatever, I don't care. Now it really is time to go." She went over and gave him a little shove in the back.

He resisted. "What's the hurry? Not your best effort, by the way." He waved the shortbread in the air. "Anyway, gotta have a slash. I drank too much to celebrate with the guys."

She felt like a sheepdog as she herded him out of the room and called out as he closed the bathroom door, "Put the seat down when you're finished."

Leaning against the wall, she waited, chewing anxiously on her thumbnail as the sound of Mark peeing went on and on. How much had he drunk? No normal bladder could hold that much, surely?

And then it happened.

The doorbell buzzed.

A swarm of bees hijacked Judith's stomach. For long, agonising seconds she hovered on the spot. Another buzz, longer this time.

Her mind raced to find a solution. If she could get Carts into her craft room before Mark exited the toilet, she'd have time for a brief explanation, enough at least to make it clear she didn't want Mark to be here. She skidded down the corridor and flung open the door, her mouth tipping into a manic smile.

Carts' face lit up. "Hi."

Judith opened her mouth, the words about to tumble out, when the toilet flushed. Carts' gaze flicked past her shoulder, a sharp crease forming between his brows. The creak of the bathroom door, then footsteps strolling along the corridor.

"You've got company." Carts' voice was strangely expressionless.

"I—oh. No. I mean yes, sort of. But he's just leaving." It was almost unbearable seeing the deep pain in Carts' eyes as they met hers. She longed to reach out, but it seemed like a huge void yawned between them and there was no way to cross it.

Then her whole body jolted as a hand landed on her shoulder. "Hallo there." Biscuity breath stirred her hair. "I'm Mark and you are…"

Carts' head jerked like he'd been punched. He swept a hand across his forehead, stepped back and almost stumbled on the stone wall next to the path. "Obviously, not good timing," he mumbled.

Yanking his collar up, he turned and strode down the path.

The words screamed inside her head. *No, no, no.*

Pitching headlong after him, she grabbed his arm as he reached the gate. "Please don't go."

Carts stared at her hand, then at her face. But it was like he didn't see her at all. "I've got the message, Judith," he said quietly.

"No, no you haven't, it's not how it looks."

He paused, hunkering into himself as if barricading against a storm. "I've made a fool of myself before in a situation like this." His mouth twisted into a bitter little smile. "And you know what I've learned?" He tugged his arm gently from her grip. "It's *always worse* than it looks."

CHAPTER 17

*W*hen Carts reached his car, he clicked the boot open, then the fuel tank, and finally set off the alarm as he fumbled madly with the remote.

"Fuck, fuck, *fuck!*" The words spluttered out through gritted teeth as he finally managed to stop the beeping and flashing.

Inside the car, he sat shaking uncontrollably. His eyelids pricked and he dashed the back of his hand angrily against his lashes.

Just twenty minutes ago he'd believed that he was invincible. As though some mysterious forces of nature had suddenly aligned and for once everything in the universe was comprehensible. He'd left his parents' place confident that Avery was okay, that Mum understood, and that little idiot Duke had bean taught a valuable lesson.

He'd got the message across, without violence or losing his cool.

And he'd been so fucking proud. So self-assured as he'd walked up the path to Judith's house. Because finally he, Carter Wells, knew what it meant to be a man.

And then…

Wham. Yet again he'd been slammed into a brick wall.

When that guy walked out of the bathroom he was right back in the moment when Lucy… *fuck*, it was almost the exact same scene, except Lucy's personal trainer had only been wearing a towel…

His fists crushed the steering wheel and he ground his teeth into his cheek to stop himself from weeping piteously.

Suddenly the words of Roxette's "It Must Have Been Love" taunted him. Oh, the fucking irony! At the most tragic moment of his life, the lyrics of a bloody eighties song had to tunnel their way into his brain.

Yeah, it sure was over now.

There was no kidding himself about that.

He blinked back a big salty tear and stared blindly out into the quiet street. His future yawned empty in front of him; images of eating cold baked beans out of the can in his sterile little kitchen as year after year passed him by. Taking his stupid old records out of their dusty covers and playing them incessantly as the paint peeled off the garden fence and his dreams of happiness lay buried under weeds and broken pavers.

A life without Judith.

A sudden knock on the window took him by surprise. He glanced up, blinked. It *looked* like Judith, so now he guessed he could add hallucinations to the list of things wrong with his existence.

The hallucinatory Judith made a winding motion with her hand.

He rubbed his eyes this time, but she stubbornly refused to disappear. She even smiled.

Hope flared in his chest as he found himself groping for the electric window button.

The window slid down. A little. Then jammed. Damn that weird hitch he'd meant to get checked at the last service. Another jab at the button sent the window up again. He tried again; down an inch.

Judith's smile turned into a lopsided grin. And he couldn't help but return it.

She made more pointy signs, which he realised meant she'd come around the other side of the car.

He grabbed a tissue from the centre console and swiped at his eyes as she made her way around the front of the car.

And then she opened the passenger door and slid in beside him.

He shifted in the seat, not sure where to look, just knowing that the space felt too small, too cramped suddenly. And she smelt fresh and citrussy, which took him back to the night they'd…

Ah, *shit.*

He scrubbed at his forehead.

"You ran away," she pointed out.

He baulked at that description. "I didn't run, exactly. I walked at speed."

"You didn't give me a chance to explain."

Carts couldn't argue with that.

He glanced up, for once wishing he hadn't cut his hair, in case she saw the glint of tears still in his eyes. "Are you two back together?"

"No. We're totally through."

He stared down at his hands and tried not to sniff. But at least a little flame of hope had re-ignited in his heart.

Her hand closed over his, steadying the tremor.

"He really is your ex?" he mumbled, studying her fingers. "Like, as in Finalised? Extinguished?"

She laughed. "Vaporised actually. I screamed at him to get out. I have literally never seen anyone move so fast." She gave a shaky laugh.

Bolder now. "Can I ask why he was there?"

She sighed. "He came round to try and borrow money off me. He's already taken all my savings."

"You are kidding!"

"No. He reckons he's developing some gaming app and wants to take it to Vegas or something. Pippa reckons he's getting into debt paying for gaming advantages. Who knows?"

"Bloody hell, what a dick."

"I agree." She stroked his hand. "Do you want to tell me what happened?"

"It would appear I stupidly walked away without giving you a chance to explain."

"No," she said gently, "I mean what happened before—to make you react like that."

Christ, her intuition was razor sharp.

He sighed. "Lucy—"

"Your last girlfriend?"

"Yeah, that one." Now she was tracing a little whorl with her finger-tips on the back of his hand. It felt divine, but it also made a lump rise in his throat again. "I thought I loved her. In all honesty, it wasn't close... we never really clicked. But anyway, we had some time apart, I'd been working long hours and she said she needed space to think. I decided, in my wisdom, that it was my fault—that I needed to be a more attentive partner. We'd talked about getting engaged at one stage and I thought that would fix it." He sucked in a deep breath. "So I went round to her place after work, with a ring I'd chosen... she opened the door and I went down on one knee and—" He heard her suck in air. "Yeah, I know, dumb right?"

"No, I was thinking that's a really romantic thing to do."

"Anyway, just as I did that, this freakin' pair of legs walks out of the bathroom at the end of the hall. And weirdly, her house is configured just like yours, toilet facing the front door and... the legs were naked 'cos the guy was only wearing a really small towel and..." He grimaced. "It was the personal trainer I'd paid for to help her overcome her insomnia problem."

"Oh, that is awful. No wonder when you saw Mark—"

"And then when he put his hand on your shoulder..."

"He did that on purpose to make mischief. I am so, so sorry it caused you pain."

"Yeah, well. I shouldn't have reacted so fast, or said what I did, but... that image just shot in front of my eyes and it's like I had no control of my body or my mind. I just reacted on auto-pilot."

"It must have seemed like history repeating itself." Judith's voice was full of compassion.

"Kind of. I'm sorry. I fucked up, didn't I? Will you forgive me?"

Gently she turned his face with her palm, gazed deeply into his eyes. "There's nothing to forgive. But please can we talk about things—like if something bothers either of us— in future."

Future. His heart leaped. They had a future?

"We've both got hurts and fears to overcome," Judith continued. "But we need to talk them through with each other. Promise me—that we'll always do that."

He looked at her, the glimmer of hope now fanning into a flame. "Do you—I mean, are you saying... that you'd like to be my girlfriend?" He pulled a face. "That sounds so freakin' adolescent, doesn't it?"

"Yes, but who cares," she murmured, pressing her forehead against his. He closed his eyes and drank in the scent of her, the nearness of her; so crazy amazing when moments ago he'd thought he'd lost her forever. "Yes, Carts, I want to be your girlfriend," she whispered.

He opened his eyes on a sigh. It felt like his whole body was releasing the tension, not only of the last hour, but of so many years. Shedding it like an old unwanted skin. When she pressed her lips against his cheek, then kissed his ear, shivers cascaded through him. And yeah, there was no denying it, the shiver had already morphed into a warm insistent hum in his groin.

He didn't know what would happen if he kissed her. If his body would let him down, and he'd have to contend with a libido like a rodeo horse, but right now he didn't care. He had to kiss her... and well, if things got tricky, he'd stop, relax and somehow, they'd work out a way to deal with it.

Together.

He lifted his hand, tipped her chin up and their gazes fused.

"You're so beautiful," he murmured and kissed her mouth as Joe Cocker, plus a full backing orchestra, launched into the opening lines of "Up Where We Belong".

JUDITH STARED at the stunning glass pendants above the desk of the Ritz Carlton Hotel.

She kept wanting to pinch herself. Because it was 11.30 at night and here they were, checking in to a river view suite, with her dressed in an outfit of Ugg boots and an old frayed cardi over her half-finished blouse, to hide the fact one arm was hanging on by a thread, and carrying a very small overnight bag.

She edged closer to Carts, who was confidently giving the receptionist his credit card, and stroked his arm. He swivelled and gave her the sexiest smile and her knees nearly buckled from under her.

They'd talked in his car. He'd told her about the awful turn of events with Avery. How he'd handled it and she'd told him how impressive that was. They'd also kissed quite a bit, until her lips felt bruised, and her belly throbbed, and she'd got a little more adventurous with her exploration.

A year of yoga had given him very toned abs, no doubting that. But when she'd let her fingers slide lower, he'd pulled back.

Her eyes sought his as his hand covered hers, stilling her movements.

"I feel like I keep doing something wrong," she said.

"No—I—" His chest rose and fell sharply. "You do everything right... that's the problem." His head was bowed but she could see his features working. "Oh fuck, you need to know, I haven't had sex with a woman for well over a year and... hell, how do I explain, I'm so turned on by you... that when you touch me... things start to move way too fast."

The words of Dr Daphne Rubekind came into Judith's mind.

Talk openly about your greatest fears.

"Is that why you only gave me pleasure the other night? Why you wouldn't let me touch you?" He didn't answer, but she persevered gently. "Why you left before I could return the favour?"

He nodded. "I've been trying some strategies to keep things in check." A grimace. "Not sure that they're working though."

She looked at his face, tight and a little miserable in the half light from the street lamp outside. "Does it matter?"

"Sorry?"

"If—" It was kind of hard, talking candidly about their sex life before it had even really started, but if they were going to get past this impasse then they had to. "If you came quickly, like, what's the big deal?" she said. "There will be plenty of other times."

His jaw went slack as if he was trying to take this in. He frowned.

"I guess so. If you were okay with that?" She'd smiled from the bottom of her heart and he'd smiled back and she'd kissed him again and then he'd said, a note of alarm in his voice, "But not here!"

"I didn't actually have the back seat of the car in mind. Besides, I don't think we'd fit."

They both laughed at that, before she asked, "Do you want to come back inside?"

He shook his head. "Maybe not after what just happened. Perhaps we could go somewhere else, at least for our first time."

"Your place?"

He pulled another face. "It's a pretty small house with thin walls—and if Solo's there—"

"Of course." She giggled. "With Polly…"

"Oh, yikes. They're on then?"

"Yep, it would seem so."

"Heck!"

They sat in silence, her mind trying to work out solutions. Did he mean for them to take a blanket down by the river? She'd go anywhere if he asked her, but if that was the case, she kind of hoped no late-night dog walkers would wander past.

"I'm thinking maybe a hotel," Carts said and her eyes widened as the idea took shape in her head.

"That could be kind of… fun!" she said.

His eyes took on a wicked gleam. "Great. Let's do this."

Giggling like a couple of teenagers wagging school, they'd made a plan and she'd run inside, leaving Carts to book over the phone. A breathless mess of excitement, she'd gathered a few things, clothes for tomorrow and toiletries, but crazily didn't feel she had time to change, so instead threw a coat over her half-made blouse.

"You look beautiful," Carts said when she plonked back in the front seat of his car, reaching over and kissing her before heading off towards the city.

After a minute she plucked up the courage to ask, "Have you… um, protection?"

He nodded and she sensed he was a little embarrassed, so she just reached over and squeezed his arm. Some things didn't need to be talked through in detail.

So here they were. At the Ritz Carlton, on Elizabeth Quay. Because, Carts had explained, he'd thought it looked amazing ever since it opened last year. "Besides," he'd added, "it's where we had our first real date."

A week ago. Really? Only a week ago. So much had happened. With Pippa, and Avery, the best orgasm of her life, a dozen red roses and *him*. He was hers, and it felt almost too good to be true.

Which was why when they stood in their suite with the great big king-size bed and the sweeping panoramic views of the river, she had to say to him, "Could you pinch me please? To check this is real."

It was more a caress than a pinch, but it would do.

They looked at the bed and then at each other and grinned.

"We should check if we fit," Carts said, with an eyebrow waggle.

Her lips quirked. "Let's," she agreed. Grabbing her hand, he ordered, "One... two... three... go!" and together they launched onto the mattress, laughing as their faces hit the feathery pillows. "Okay, turn round and lie absolutely straight."

They turned and lay flat on their backs, fingers linked together, staring at the ceiling and wiggling their toes. "I'm off the end," Carts said.

"I fit. Just," Judith countered. "But then you are taller than me."

"Doesn't matter," he said, turning on his side and scooping her into his arms. "It means we'll have to snuggle up more." They curled into each other, faces close enough for their noses to touch and their breath to mingle. Suddenly serious now, she gulped and gently traced a finger round the angle of his cheekbones, the line of his jaw, and across his mouth. How sensitive those lips were, how expressive. He blinked at her, long eyelashes sweeping down and when he opened them again, his eyes were as clear as the night sky outside.

In turn, he stroked the hair away from her face and kissed her. First her forehead, then each eyelid, her cheeks next and finally, her lips.

It was a languorous kiss at first, explorative and gentle, as if they had all the time in the world. His tongue swept her upper lip, then her lower one and Judith gave a little shiver. She let her lips mould to his and coaxed with her tongue, until he opened to her and she felt his hands tangle in her hair and the kiss deepened and became hot and urgent.

Judith pulled at his shirt, tugged it out of his pants. He laughed, a little nervous, deep and husky. His eyes darkened. She let her hand roam across the skin of his belly then snuck it over his pants to shape the hard length of him.

He flinched.

"Is this okay?" she asked. "Or too much?"

"A little too much right now." The words came out slightly strangled. She shifted, letting him have space to breathe and stroking her fingertips softly over his shoulders and pecs, a place she hoped was safe enough.

"Why don't we undress at least?" she suggested after a while. "And see what happens."

He looked at her, uncertainty mixed with desire. "I'm not sure I'm going to cope with seeing you naked. I'm teetering right on the edge here."

"Just for your info, I'm nervous too. I have one breast that's bigger than the other." She giggled into his neck. "You only got to one the other night, the smaller one, before—"

"I will love each of them equally," he said with a reverence that made her skin goosebump with joy.

"Oh, thank you. So, you see, we don't have to be perfect. Either of us. But this, you know, *this*... is perfect—just us, being here, together."

"More than perfect. And you *are* perfect."

"Lopsided but perfect."

"Perfect. End of story."

They lay still for five minutes, maybe longer, exploring each other with a light touch and long sighs.

Finally, Judith decided to nudge things along. "How about we turn the lights off, take our clothes off and get under the covers—no major expectations or anything," she added as she sensed his spine stiffen.

She saw the relief sweep his face. "You always have such good ideas."

She stroked his hair. "Being with you brings out my best ideas," she said softly. "Let's do this, sexy man."

He laughed and this time, she was sure that deep huskiness held more confidence.

"Lights out," he said.

Judith obligingly flicked the switch.

CHAPTER 18

*C*lothes shed, Carts lay very still under the sheet. He dared cast a look at her silhouetted against the window, the outline of one tip-tilted breast, the line of her shoulder and curve of her hip. Her long slender legs.

He felt her body indent the mattress, the waft of air as she pulled back the sheet and climbed in next to him.

Then her head was on his shoulder and with a sigh her hands were exploring over his naked chest, her warm breath on his neck, her thighs brushing the hairs on his.

He turned into her and his cock bobbed hard against the swell of her belly. It was nigh on impossible to focus on anything but how much he wanted to be inside her.

She feathered kisses across his cheek towards his mouth.

"Don't kiss me." He arched his neck, gritted his teeth. "I mean, do kiss me, just not for a moment."

"We'll go at your pace," she whispered.

They lay still, holding each other tight while desire throbbed through every cell of his body.

After a while Judith murmured, "Do you want to…"

He almost yelped, "Now?"

He sensed the smile in her words. "Well, I'm already one up on you in the orgasm stakes." She gave a husky little laugh. "And we've got all night for second helpings."

All night. Jesus, the sheer amazingness of it made his mouth dry up.

And really, that was all the encouragement he needed. He found the packet of condoms he'd left on the bedside table, tore it open and sheathed himself.

When he turned back to her, Judith reached for him, and he nestled between her legs and drew in a ragged breath as her breasts and hips moulded into him.

He wasn't used to this. He was used to having to wait, to defer, to ensure he gave pleasure first, not just selfishly took his own.

He sighed deeply, burying his face in her neck, drinking in her scent.

And then he accepted the truth of it. It didn't matter what happened next. It didn't need to fit some blueprint of the first time. Because after the first time, he knew now that there would be a next time, the chance to explore each other's bodies at leisure, to get to know each other's wants and needs.

Carts gave himself up to the moment.

She guided him gently, her touch sensitive to how easily triggered he was down there right now, and gingerly he moved so that he nudged her entrance.

He bit his lip, closed his eyes, braced on his elbows, so as not to crush her breasts with his weight. She let out a deep sigh, and the sweet hot wetness of her welcomed him.

He stilled, breathing heavily.

"Would you mind—just—staying still a moment?"

She stroked his hair, whispered words of encouragement in his ear. An ache of tenderness joined the lust in his groin.

Then her mouth found his and she kissed him, gently, with parted lips, keeping her tongue out of the equation so as not to turn the temperature up any higher, while he remained clasped tight within her and... yes, breathe... yes... he was going okay... he was... he could hold out... he could...

Until with a little moan, Judith changed the rules, deepening the kiss,

157

throwing her legs around his hips, sweeping him along with her rhythm, taking him deep inside her and oh god, he couldn't stop the movement of his hips in unison, could not... He was being carried by a wave so powerful that... nope, nope, heaven COULD NOT WAIT.

He came with absolute abandon, his whole body tossed around by the rip tide of his orgasm. He knew that he shouted out words of delight and amazement, knew that her name played a central role, but not if any of it was coherent. When he collapsed against her, spent and blissed out, Judith crooned sweet nothings in his ear until his ragged breathing steadied and he was certain he'd been reborn and laid on a bed of goose-down sewn together with golden thread.

He had no idea how long they lay like that, their legs and arms entwined, his head nestled into the dip of her collarbone.

Except somewhere in there he had the presence of mind to remove the condom, which he did with far more ease than he'd put it on. Amazing what a blinding orgasm could do to your anatomy.

Back in her arms a moment later, he said, "I tried to hold out, but then you did... that thing with your hips... like, how do you do that?"

"Trade secret." She giggled and added, "I'm actually flattered you couldn't hold out."

"Grrrr, you're taking advantage of my weakness—and you're not going to win."

It was payback time. With the issue of his trigger-happy dick out the way and his limbs feeling as loose and relaxed as pulled toffee, it was time to focus on the woman he loved.

Loved?

Yes. Loved. He loved Judith Mellors... He loved her and he was darn sure she loved him.

And even if it was too early to say those words out loud, the realisation would have knocked his socks off if he'd been wearing any, which thankfully he wasn't, because making love with your socks on was totally *fucked*.

He realised now that he'd been presented with the real McCoy, that his clumsy attempts at love before had been mere play acting, hoping that those mediocre relationships would make him feel he belonged in a world that was too bewildering... too cruel.

But with Judith he didn't have to pretend. She saw beneath the awkward façade to the real him. And she liked what she saw. All the imperfections; his unruly hair and bony ankles... and most importantly... his fragile heart. And she wanted all of them.

All of *him*.

Suddenly ridiculously happy, he let his fingers trail down until they met the swell of her breast, her taut nipple. When she gave a breathy sigh he whispered, "You didn't honestly think we'd finished?" And when she turned her body into him he became braver still. "Do you think it's safe to turn the lights back on?"

CARTS' fingers on her breast, coaxing her nipple into a hard little peak was incredibly erotic to watch, and like a she-cat tempting her mate, she licked her lips. The ambient light from the bedside lamp accentuated the swell of his shoulder and bicep, his firm pecs, the dusting of dark hairs across his chest, the chocolate brown of his nipples, his long sensitive fingers.

He really had no idea how beautiful he was.

In another brain-space she'd pick up a pencil and draw the lines of his torso, shadow in the play of muscles on his chest and abs, but no, oh no, not right now.

Because his hands were playing her like an instrument, his attention focused on every reaction, like he was listening for the beat and cadence of her body to tell him what his next note should be.

He was a musician alright, maybe not in the same way as his sister, but he was a maestro of touch.

"Nice?" he asked, his smoky gaze holding hers as his hand cupped her breast, his thumb sweeping gently back and forth over her nipple. Her lips quivered a silent yes, and he smiled as his hand strayed over her ribs, smoothed over her belly to meet the curve of her hips and dipped lower still...

She arched to meet him.

When his hand slid between her legs, his fingers gently parting her and finding the bud of her clitoris, she held onto his shoulders as the tension rose inside her, a symphony of longing, building to a crescendo.

He stroked, he coaxed, he strummed her so expertly that she had no choice but to go where his touch led.

"Kiss me," she begged, knowing how close she was.

She wanted him inside her again. Would he be ready? She reached down and with satisfaction felt the hard ridge of his erection.

"Another condom." It was a demand, her building orgasm overpowering any residual niceness.

Carts obliged.

"What do you want?" Those words were almost enough to make her come on the spot. The need inside her quickened.

She had to be on top.

Flinging back the covers, she delighted in the glory of him, his narrow hips and the v of dark hair that arrowed down to where he was hard and proud and ready for her again.

"Okay?" he rasped.

She nodded, hands splayed on his chest, feeling the base of his penis against her sex. She manoeuvred until he was positioned just right and moved herself up and down the length of him.

Her head kicked back as his hand moved between them, touching her, just right.

And now there was more than sweet music, there was a crescendo building of their breath rising and quickening, of his murmured praise of her beauty, of the dampness gathering on his brows and the darkening of his eyes.

She saw his jaw tighten as she clamped hard around him in the moment just before her orgasm. And then it was like they were tipped over, tumbling, holding on to one another, not knowing where they would land but safe because they were in this together.

Freefalling.

Some time later, lying against his chest with his arms around her, she asked, "Do you think we made a lot of noise?"

"Probably." He kissed the top of her head. "Does it matter?"

No, it didn't, she realised. She really didn't care if anyone in the neighbouring room complained about the sounds coming from room 224, or if a staff member walking past to deliver room service heard her scream out Carts' name. Or whether there would be tell-tale stains on the sheets.

None of it mattered.

All that mattered was this man and her.

And making sure they made love again before the sun came up.

THE FIRST THING he noticed when he woke was that his feet were toasty warm.

He wiggled his toes and immediately felt a return pressure.

Then something brushed against the sole of his foot.

Toes, he realised. Attached to a foot that wasn't his. Judith's foot. Delight arrowed all the way up his leg in a wave of goosebumps. He lay still as the foot spidey walked up to his calf, and then a leg was thrown languorously over his, bringing soft skin and the brush of her pubes into direct contact with his butt.

Holy fuck. His cock was standing to attention.

With a smile splitting his face, he turned around and snuggled in to her, drinking in the musty scent and still sleepy eyes, the little freckle above her left eyebrow, the fairness of her lashes at the tips. He was getting familiar with it all.

Her gaze was luminous, like sunshine breaking through morning mist.

"Hello, you."

"Good morning, you."

She aimed a kiss at his lips, but he pressed them tight and muttered, "Morning breath."

"Don't care," she said, and kissed him.

Just as he was about to give in and open to her, his phone rang. He scrabbled for it on the bedside table.

161

"Aaron," he mouthed at her, and with a sigh she snuggled into his shoulder and he flung an arm around her and oh, how good did that feel right now.

"Hi there." He liked the way his greeting sounded kind of deep and gravelly.

"Mate, you never called me last week."

"Sorry, things got a bit hectic."

"Everything okay?" Aaron sounded slightly worried.

'Everything's—perfect."

"You sound like a man who got lucky last night," Aaron observed, rather astutely.

At that Judith let out a giggle.

A pause, and then, more circumspect on the end of the line, "Whoops, obviously not alone."

A small, sweet voice from the vicinity of his shoulder said, "Say hello to Aaron and Alice from me."

A warm glow bracketed his heart. Here she was, lying naked in his arms, introducing herself. How much clearer could she make it she was his woman?

"Judith says to say hi to you and Alice." He felt his chest puffing with pride.

"Say hi back from us."

"Tell them I know Polly," Judith whispered loudly; he repeated it. "Judith knows Polly, they work together."

He could hear Aaron relaying this fact to Alice in the background. He switched his phone to hands-free so Judith could hear as Alice's voice piped up. "Oh, Judith the occupational therapist on Echidna Ward, right? Hi Judith."

"Hi, Alice." Judith waved at the phone. "Can you see me?"

"No, you don't need to turn the camera on," Carts said hastily.

"Got that." Aaron's voice held a smile. "Anyway, we've got some news."

"You're pregnant."

Aaron laughed outright. "Give us a year or so more freedom, mate. No, we're coming home early."

"Seriously!" Carts' heart bounced in his chest. He knew he'd missed them both, but now it hit him just how much. He sat up and Judith wriggled up with him so now they both had their backs against the headboard.

He glanced at her, her eyes wide with excitement as she gave him a thumbs up.

"That's fantastic. When?" he asked.

"In a week. Alice is getting homesick and I'm wanting to have some time free before I start my new job in Legal Aid."

"That's brilliant mate."

"Would you be able to meet us at the airport? We arrive on Sunday."

"Love to."

"Our flight gets in mid-afternoon, I'll text you the details. And... feel free to bring Judith with you."

Carts mouthed, "Want to?" and she nodded vigorously. No hesitation meant no hesitation that they would be together in a week.

He knew he didn't need to feel insecure, but the habit had been years in the making. He guessed it would take more than a week to shed it completely. By now Judith had slipped out of bed and as he finished his conversation and said his goodbyes, he stared longingly at her departing figure.

He wanted her so badly again he was at risk of panting.

He didn't have to wait long. She padded back a moment later, a white towel loosely wrapped around her body. She threw another one on the bed.

Brows waggled seductively over saucy eyes.

"What do you reckon to trying out the spa bath?" She licked her lips, turned and gave him a sexy as hell hip wiggle.

Faster than a speeding bullet, Carts shot off the bed, grabbed the towel and followed her.

A WHILE LATER, after proving that two people over six foot could not only fit into the—admittedly giant—spa bath, but also make love in it without too much water spillage, they dried each other tenderly, dressed and headed down to a buffet breakfast in the restaurant.

"I don't think I've eaten this much in my life," Judith said as she finally finished stuffing her face with bacon and eggs and pastries, and sat back rubbing the hard little drum of her stomach. "It feels very decadent, like I've been at a Roman feast." She let out a big contented sigh. "This has been the best... most amazing night. I've never done anything like it before. And to be honest, I've never really had anyone I've wanted to do it with." She glanced at him to see the warmth in his brown eyes. "Until now."

"Same." He reached over and took her hand in his.

"We *are* getting adventurous in our old age," she laughed.

"Bungee jumping here we come."

"Make that a tandem skydive."

"I'll lock it in for our first anniversary." He looked covertly from under his lashes, and she weaved her fingers into his.

"I'd like that," she said.

They sat for a moment, well fed and contented, then Carts asked, "Do you want to do something after breakfast?"

She hesitated, and he immediately picked up on it. "You've got other plans?"

She sighed. "I have to try and get Mum and Pippa talking."

A look of sudden comprehension dawned on his face. "Oh, christ, I'm sorry I forgot, with us and you know... Do you want to tell me what happened?"

With the whirlwind of events last night, there hadn't been time to talk about Friday night. Nor, frankly, had she wanted to. She'd wanted to forget her family's woes hanging over her. But now she explained the whole messy situation. Carts listened, his head inclined toward her, eyes intent, wincing when she explained how Pip had stormed off. "Oh jeesh," he added a couple of times. It felt so good to talk about it that the leaden lump around her heart softened. She realised how much anxiety she'd always carried around with regard to Mum and Pippa. And as she talked, memories surfaced; of the times she'd listened to Pippa crying when Mum was too exhausted to go to her and Dad was working. How when she couldn't bear it anymore, she'd go to the fridge, take out Pip's bottle, drag a chair to the microwave and stand on it to warm it, then struggle to pick up Pip's distressed little body from the cot.

"So why is it up to you to get them talking again?" Carts asked when she'd finished.

Her brow pleated as she sought for the words. "Because... because... I always have. It's kind of ingrained in me..." She flicked a strand of hair over her shoulder, gave a nervous laugh. "Maybe I'm worried that if I stop caring as much, I'll end up being one of those people who barge to the front of queues and walk past homeless people without blinking an eye."

"That would never happen," Carts said softly. "But sometimes caring too much means people lean on us when they should be fixing their own problems."

She looked at his thoughtful expression, loving the wisdom that emerged when he relaxed into being truly himself. "You're right, and I get that, logically. At work I know where to draw the line. But with Mum and Pip it all gets scrambled in my head. As though if I don't sort it out something awful will happen."

"Like when your mum disappeared when you were little and you didn't know why?"

She gulped, nodded. When he spoke, Carts' voice was full of compassion. "All the muddy shit from the past, eh?"

"Yes!" She let out a big breath, surprised and delighted that he got it. "That's exactly how it feels, all the shit from the past messing up my head."

"I know that shit," Carts said. "It's the reason I let my boss treat me like a turd on his shoe, even though I know I'm the best performer in the team. It's why I never ask for a pay rise, or go for promotions. Even when the bullying stopped at school, even when I made friends, deep inside I still didn't believe... that I deserved..." He hesitated, the fingers of his other hand curling around his napkin and turning it into a tightly scrunched ball.

"That you deserved...?" she prompted gently.

"To be happy." His knuckles whitened and he glanced up at her, eyes clouded. "With Lucy, I knew in my heart it was over between us, but it was like I wanted to whack myself over the head with a two by four plank. Even as I went and chose that engagement ring, there was a great big sign flashing in my brain. *Don't do this.* And then I did it anyway; like I was determined to prove to myself I was no good. That I deserved to be kicked in the teeth. And that's exactly what happened. I let all that shitty stuff from when I was bullied affect my judgement over Lucy."

She wound her fingers around his, brought his hand to her lips and kissed it. "And then with you—" His voice cracked a little. "If you hadn't come running after me… because in my head it was like, of course, this is how it is, this is what you get in life Carts, mate, this is what you deserve. It felt weirdly right."

"But you were so wrong."

He nodded. "I was. And I'm so glad you didn't let me leave." They sat holding hands in the companionable silence of two people who totally got each other before Carts said, "So tell me, what's the major issue with Pippa and your mum?"

"Where to begin?" She sighed heavily. "They've each got so much baggage. Mum feels guilty because she had post-natal depression, but then she also withdraws because she finds Pippa's energy too intense. But to Pippa, that means Mum doesn't care. So she tries to force Mum into a reaction. Every single time. And it always, *always* backfires." He squeezed her hand in simple acknowledgement. "And then, guess who runs around to fix it all up?" She pointed her other hand at her chest. "Moi."

"What do you do?"

"I call and I cajole and I organise everyone to come to tea and… I bake brownies." She heard herself laugh, hollow and mirthless. "Until they start talking again, but they never sort it out, not really. It builds up like those rock formations in caves. Drip, drip, drip. And now…" She sighed. "This is the big one, the hardest for both of them."

"But they do love each other?"

"Yes, yes, of course. We *all* love each other, but we're one of those families who don't know how to show it."

"How many families really do? How many families really talk to each

166

other about the hard stuff? I know mine don't. Dad hides in his study, worrying himself sick about his work, Mum teaches her ring off to kids who don't want to learn the piano. I didn't tell them I was being bullied, not until years later. Now, Avery can't talk to Mum anymore. They rub each other up the wrong way constantly."

"Sounds like Mum and Pippa." She took a big breath. She needed to tell him the rest.

"Mum had a terrible childhood. Her family belonged to a fundamental church. The kind where if you did anything the church didn't approve of you'd roast in hell for eternity. Strictly no sex before marriage, no university education for women, as little contact with the outside world as possible. You had to marry someone from the church. They'd lined up a church elder in his forties for Mum to marry on her eighteenth birthday."

"That's terrible."

Yeah, I know. Awful. With the help of a woman whose daughter Mum knew from school, Mum fled to Perth. And met Dad, and Dad's always kind of sheltered her. Mum did okay with parenting me and Luke, and then Pip was born and it was a difficult birth and Pip had colic and screamed for hours and that's when Mum got badly depressed."

"And you learned to cook," he said softly. When their eyes met, the infinite kindness in his made her want to cry.

"Yes." She gulped and gave him a tight little smile. "I just wanted everything to be okay. Everyone to be happy."

"Of course you did. What seven-year-old wouldn't want their family to be happy?" He paused. "But maybe now it's time to focus on what makes *you* happy."

Without hesitation she said, "This," and leaned over and kissed him.

"Yes," said Carts. "This." And kissed her back.

And even though there was a table of piled up plates between them, this time, she sensed no resistance, no pulling away.

Just his warm lips loving hers.

CHAPTER 19

*C*arts heard the flute and piano duet even before he opened the gate. Mozart, he could tell that much; a sonata he guessed, but that was about the extent of his knowledge. What mattered was he'd heard Mum and Avery playing it often enough.

Together.

As the notes drifted through the open window, a sense of wellbeing enveloped him.

Okay, given the choice he'd probably still be wandering around Perth with Judith, if she hadn't had a job to do. "I have to tell them they need to sort out their differences. That I can't be the go-between anymore," she'd said emphatically. "And then I'm going to draw up an IOU agreement and send it to Mark."

"Do you need any accountant speak thrown in?" He'd happily write the little fuckwit a jargon-filled IOU, on Pearson's letterhead.

"I'll call you if I get stuck."

And when she'd smiled at him, it had felt like they were a team. Like he had found an ally who would shield his back while he shielded hers. Together they were stronger. Wasn't that how it was supposed to be when you were in a great relationship? Better together than apart?

Skirting around the house now, he quietly let himself in through the

168

doors of Mum's music room. A surprising sight greeted him; not only were Mum and Avery playing, but Dad was sitting in the wing chair in a corner, listening intently.

Dad was usually off doing his own thing in his office, stooped over his oak desk with its green-shaded desk lamp, a worried hand stroking his bald head as he marked student papers or prepped for his next lecture.

"Hi there, Carter." Dad looked up with a bright smile. No criss-cross of creases on his forehead.

Mum and Avery stopped for a brief second, but Carts shook his head. "That's beautiful, keep going." He pulled up a chair next to Dad, and seamlessly, they started up where they'd left off.

Avery's face was pale, but her eyes no longer had that haunted look about them as she wrinkled them over the top of her flute in acknowledgement.

Mum looked happy and relaxed. Like suddenly everything in the world was back in its rightful place.

As for his dad—Carts cast a perplexed glance at his father. With one leg crossed over the other, his foot tapped to the rhythm. And his lips were tilted upwards in a smile, which was as rare as hen's teeth when it came to Dad.

Carts drew up a chair and listened until the piece was over. Dad applauded with gusto. Carts joined in.

Avery grinned and gave a little bow, then placed her flute reverently back in its case.

He went and gave her a hug. "How are you feeling?" he asked as she nestled into his embrace.

"Okay," she said, a little guarded, then pulled back and glanced at Mum. "But I'm not going to school tomorrow."

"Yes you are," Mum said with a touch of steel in her voice.

"Not if you insist on taking me." Avery pouted. "I know you'll say something to Zammy."

"Dead right I will," Mum answered. "I want that boy's address. If his mother knew…"

"Seewhatimean!" Avery squealed indignantly. "I wish I'd never told you. You'll do something embarrassing. I can sort this myself, Mum."

"How about if I take you to school?" Dad said quietly. Avery's mouth fell open and her eyes widened. "Really, seriously, you would?"

"Absolutely. I'd love to." Dad stood up and rubbed his hands together in a gesture Carts remembered from times when he'd take them all off on an expedition to find fossils, or out on the boat to point out the different kinds of algae. "Let's lighten up a bit. Shall I put the kettle on for a cup of tea, Mrs Wells?"

Mum put the piano lid down and the atmosphere relaxed a tad. The subject of Zammy was closed, at least for now. "Yes, the cake's in the cupboard, second shelf down. Be careful of the icing."

Carts and Avery both cast identical puzzled looks at their parents, and Carts racked his brain. No, it wasn't anyone's birthday. Dad's was still two months away, and Mum's was on Boxing Day. Avery, he'd never forget, came kicking and screaming into the world on the third day of January.

While Dad was off clattering cups in the kitchen, Mum said to Avery, "That was seamless, love. Nice and even, no wavering on the longer notes."

Avery gave a grudging smile. "What's the cake for?"

Mum returned a secretive smile. "You'll see."

When Dad came in he was balancing a big tray with cups and plates and an iced sponge cake with a plaque that read, "Congratulations".

It all seemed a bit inappropriate, after Avery's night from hell.

Dad poured the tea, sliced the cake and handed out portions.

Carts eyed his piece. How was he ever going to fit it in after his huge breakfast? "Mum, this looks amazing, did you make it?"

"I did. It's an idiot-proof Andrea Blake, I saved it from the Sunday paper."

Carts grinned. Aaron's stepmum's recipes were in the paper every week. He'd never thought to try cooking one himself, but with Judith to guide him… the thought created a starburst of joy in his chest.

"Well," said Dad, grinning and wrinkling his tattooed eyebrows. Doing that always showed them up as being fake, but hey, what did any of that matter? It was a person's imperfections that made them special, after all. "I have some news. I had the nod that I've landed the head of department position. It will be announced on Monday."

"Oh Dad, that's amazing!" Avery pitched herself at her father and he hugged her.

"I'm so sorry sweetheart. I've been an absent father lately. Worried about being made redundant. I should have paid more attention to what was going on for you. But anyhow, looks like we'll be able to afford your year in Paris, now."

"No!" Avery recoiled and stepping back, nearly tripped over the rug. Carts caught her, and felt her body go rigid. "No, I don't want to."

"But darling…" Mum protested.

"No. You don't understand. Mum. Dad." She looked from one of her parents to the other, panic-stricken. "I'm not ready to leave home. I don't want to go that far away. Like yesterday, I thought I was ready to go to that party and be… an adult and all that stuff, and I couldn't handle any of it." She pressed shaky fingers into her eyes. "I just want to go at my own pace. Grow up the way I want to, not feel all this pressure all the time. It makes me so anxious."

"Maybe we should talk about this later, when you've got over the shock of last night," Mum soothed.

Avery shook her head. "I've made up my mind." Her jaw set. "I'm not going to Paris. I'll apply to the Academy of Performing Arts here in Perth, but I am not going that far away from home."

Carts placed a steadying arm around her trembling shoulders. She never needed to feel bad about being a homebody. Avery blinked up at him through teary eyes. "I don't want to leave you, and Mum and Dad. Why does everyone want to push me to grow up before I'm ready?"

Mum opened her mouth, possibly to point out that no-one had forced Avery to go to Zammy's party in a scrap of sparkly material the size of a tea towel, but luckily Dad stepped in. "Well said, sweetheart." He frowned hard at Mum. "If you want to study here, of course you can. There's always post-grad overseas—when you're older. And I, for one, would have to say we've got some of the best places in the world to study, right here in Perth."

Carts felt Avery's body uncoil bit by bit. Her mouth tilted at the corners.

Mum sighed. "But it's such an opportunity, darling. Why don't you at least think about—"

"Rosemary, don't live your life vicariously through our daughter," Dad said sternly.

Mum looked quite taken aback.

"You pushed Avery to apply for that scholarship, and if you want my reading of the situation, it's because you missed out."

Mum nibbled on her piece of cake, choosing not to catch anyone's eye.

"Admit it, Rosemary."

Mum huffed and put her plate down. "Hmmm, okay, yes, I would have loved the opportunity if my family could have afforded it." She sighed. "And then I met you... well, no regrets, you dear old thing." She looked at Avery and smiled. "I have to say as it got closer, I have thought maybe it's not the right thing for you. And I know I'd miss you terribly, sweetheart."

"Even though we fight?" Avery asked, licking a blob of icing off her finger.

"Isn't that what parents are supposed to do with their teenage kids?" Mum laughed, a tad ruefully.

After this, they all sat and chatted about what Dad's new job would entail and ate more of the cake. Despite his breakfast feast with Judith, Carts proved yet again there was always a sweet spot left. Quite a large one, he decided, as he took a second slice.

When Dad mentioned the substantial pay rise that went with the position, Carts had a sudden thought. "Why don't you treat yourself to something, Dad? You've turned into a complete workaholic these past few years and it can't be good for your health."

"I know I have." Dad's shoulders sagged. "Work just seems to demand more and more out of you these days."

"You could always think about buying another boat," Carts suggested. "Second-hand, surely that would be affordable?"

A slow smile dawned on Dad's face. He looked at his wife. "Rosemary, do you think... something like we used to have, just to fossick around on the river at weekends?"

"Oh, yes Dad, yes." Avery clapped her hands together. "That would be so cool. I could take Bec and my friends from the orchestra out on it."

Dad laughed. "Impromptu concerts on the river you reckon?"

Mum said thoughtfully, as she got up to clear the plates, "It would be nice to do more as a family. And, yes, I do think you need something other than work, Adrian. I guess it would be good for all of us to spend more time relaxing. It feels like years since we've focused on enjoying life."

"And how about you, Carter?" Dad turned to him. "You've always talked about learning to sail. How about me teaching you the basics, then getting some lessons?"

A delighted grin spread across Carts' face. "You bet!"

AFTER SHE LEFT CARTS, Judith got busy.

Seated at her desk in her craft room, the place she always felt at her best, she sat and typed up an IOU agreement to send to Mark. Terms: one month to have the full $3000 back in her account.

Not. Negotiable.

If that didn't work, she'd take Carts up on his offer to help with something more formal. But for now, she wanted to be the one to state her position clearly. On her own terms.

As she sent the email, she felt immensely pleased with herself. Rome wasn't built in a day and all that, but at least she'd started to lay down the foundations.

Afterwards, she changed into jeans and sneakers, tugged a baggy jumper over her head, and coiled her long hair into a bun.

Then she headed for her parents' house.

When she got there, she let herself in with her key. Dad was sitting in the living room watching a replay of yesterday's footy match. Mum was nowhere to be seen.

Her heart dropped. "Where's Mum?"

"She's not got up yet."

"How is she?"

"Subdued. But she'll be glad to see you when she wakes up." Dad flicked the top off his beer can with a fizz. "Why don't you grab a beer and sit and watch the footy with me?"

She hadn't had a beer in years, and she wouldn't have a clue who was doing what in footy, but the sudden urge to just sit with her dad was overwhelming.

"Sure, is there a cold one in the fridge?"

"Yep, second shelf, grab yourself a glass."

She got the beer and was just about to get a glass out of the cabinet when she halted. Why did she always need a glass? She tugged at the ring pull and cold beer fizzed out of the top. She licked it off and let the bubbles fizz on her tongue. She went over to the sofa, sat down next to Dad, crossed one leg over the other, and slurped loudly from the can.

He laughed.

"That's not like you."

She shot him a little smile. "Well, people can change, right?"

They sat and watched the game and she even found herself getting excited along with Dad as he barracked for his team. It used to be Dad and Pippa, shouting at the TV, both wearing their green and purple beanies and scarves, while Mum and Judith hid together upstairs, sewing, and Luke did his own thing. Poor Dad, he'd always hoped Luke would be into footy, but Luke had not been sporty at all, much to Dad's disappointment.

Parents and kids. So many expectations. So many disappointments. Unless you just accepted each other for who you were.

She took another sip of beer and asked, "How are you feeling—about Pip's news?"

He pursed his lips and shook his head. "You know, I've always suspected. Never said anything to your mum, but I often wondered..."

"You did?" She turned and looked at him, jaw slack. Dad, who always seemed oblivious to anything but building contracts and plans, who always changed the channel when anything about sex came on the TV. She hadn't even twigged, and Dad had always suspected Pip was gay!

"We men are not as unobservant as you sometimes think." He winked and took a swig of his beer. "But, you know, I kept my own counsel. Your mum… She's a very reserved, private person, and doesn't like to talk about stuff like this. I respect that because, well, you know, everything she went through… we understand each other."

He turned his eyes back to the screen. "Oh jeesh, will you just look at that, what a waste of an opportunity!" He took another mouthful of beer. "As for you, luv," he patted her knee, "it's about time you stopped rescuing this family, eh?"

Judith could hardly believe her ears. This was radical. Dad had everything all worked out, every one of his children sussed, and she'd never, ever realised.

But still she had to check she'd heard right. "You think I do that?"

"Yep. Ever since you were a wee small thing." He sighed. "You've always been bloody good at it. I should have stepped in and made sure you didn't look after your mum so much, but… life was hectic and stressful in those days. No excuses, but I guess what I'm saying is, parents aren't perfect, they make mistakes. But now, sweetheart, it's time you put your needs first. Grab some happiness of your own."

"Oh Dad," Judith said, a little catch in her voice. "That's exactly what I intend to do."

There was the sound of footsteps upstairs, and the toilet flushed. Dad's eyes shifted to the ceiling. "She's awake."

Judith got up and made for the door.

"Before you go," Dad said, "your mum and Pip. They're going to have to sort this out between themselves."

"I know."

Mum wasn't in her bedroom, or in the spare room where she did her craft. Judith poked her head in. Everything was neatly arranged, each drawer carefully labelled, Mum's new loom taking pride of place—she'd recently taken up weaving—the neatly twisted balls of yarn in hues of mauves and blues sitting beside it, waiting for her next project.

Instead Judith found her sitting in Pip's old room, on the bed.

She steeled herself. "Hi, Mum."

Mum gave her a wan smile. "Hi darling. What are you doing here?"

"I came—" She was going to say, to see how you are, but she knew how her mum would be. "I'm here to ask you to talk to Pippa."

Mum looked away swiftly, her features tightening. Judith went and sat next to her on the bed, and with a start realised Mum was clasping Pippa's school photo from when she was twelve. Before the spray painting started. The excited grin, her big front teeth, the freckles, the bright halo of her hair.

Rambunctious, glorious Pippa.

Mum shook her head. "I don't understand her. I should, shouldn't I?" Her tone was perplexed. "A mother should understand her daughter. I understand you, but I've never been able to work out Pippa." She huffed out a little laugh. "Remember when she was still no more than four, she'd jump out from behind the sofa with that purple wig on and one of those awful party whistle things and shout 'Invasion from Mars!' and Luke would call her the little alien. That's how it used to feel. Like a little alien landed in our life."

Judith smiled. "That's Pip, that's just how she's made."

"I worry about her," Mum said quietly. "The way she wears her heart on her sleeve, opens her mouth and blurts out her whole life. She leaves herself open to people abusing her."

"That's not going to happen, not to Pip."

Mum's fingers stroked the photo. "People will turn this against her."

Gently Judith said, "Does it bother you, her being gay?"

"No." Mum sighed. "No, honestly, it's not about that." She looked at Judith out of cloudy grey eyes. "Shaz seems a lovely girl, they can do what they want to in private, but they need to know that people *judge*."

"The world isn't the one you grew up in, Mum. It's not full of people who preach hell and damnation."

"I think you're wrong. I think there's lots of horrible, cruel people out there."

Judith took a deep breath. "If there are people who don't accept Pip for being gay, you know what? She'll cope with that. She's strong."

Mum shook her head "You don't understand what it's like to be ostracised, Judith. I do."

"I don't, Mum, you're right. But what I *do* know is you had immense courage. To leave your community, your family, everything you knew, your whole life, and move to a strange city where you knew no-one. Because you believed in a better life, where you were free to be you. You and Pippa are more alike than you think."

"I wasn't a good mother to her."

"You had post-natal depression. That's an illness, Mum, not a choice."

"But… I didn't bond with her… I left you to—"

Judith put her finger to her lips. "So it wasn't perfect. What family is? You need to trust that Pippa can look after herself, and most importantly, celebrate that she's found happiness."

They both gazed at the picture of Pip.

"Look at that hair." Mum's voice held a hint of a smile. "She's always had so much fire in her belly. She'd never back down from anything."

"Yeah, I know." A moment's silence. "You can both get past this, you know," Judith said. "But you have to start talking to each other. Please call her, Mum."

Mum shook her head. "If I say one wrong word she'll jump down my throat. You know I can't handle her shouting at me."

"She only shouts because she wants to be heard. And Mum, honestly, it's not just Pippa. It's you going into your cave. Doing the silent treatment. I can't be the one who sorts you both out. I can't bake brownies and invite you round and carry the conversation while you avoid eye contact and Pippa grunts like a sulky bear. You need to work it through with each other."

Mum snagged her lower lip between her teeth.

"Phone her, Mum. She needs to know you love her, that you accept her and her relationship with Shaz."

"I will— soon."

"Why not today?"

Mum's chin retracted, her eyes wide. "Oh darling, I'm not sure I can deal with Pippa this soon."

Judith firmed her heart. "No time like the present, Mum; it's the only place we can ever change things."

Mum looked ready to prevaricate but Judith gently took the photo out of her hands and put it back on the dressing table. "Why don't you show me those new wools I saw next to your loom? They're the most amazing shades. Where did you get them from?"

As she left half an hour later, having talked through warps and wefts, and how the new loom worked, Mum looked happier, and more relaxed. At the door, about to leave, Judith turned, and held her hand to her ear in a phone gesture.

Mum nodded. Judith was about to close the door when Mum said, "You look different."

"I'm wearing jeans."

"No, it's more than that." Mum swept her forehead with a hand, as if thinking. "You've got a glow about you."

Judith smiled. The Judith of before would have passed it off on the late afternoon light, or the new blush she'd put on. But now she took the compliment and let it nestle into her heart. "Thanks Mum."

And then she drove to the netball courts.

When she arrived, The Badass Girls were nearing the end of their Sunday practice session. It didn't take long to locate her sister's bright red head zooming up and down the court, and if she hadn't, Pippa's voice would have told her where to look. She spied Shaz a moment later, her long legs pounding up the court and *poomph*, she plopped that ball through the net with the grace and ease of a gazelle.

Judith waited on the sidelines while the team chatted with their coach and then Pippa came jogging over, wiping her face with the bottom of her shirt hem.

"Hey babe," she said. "What are you doing here?"

"I just need to have a word," Judith replied.

Pippa's expression turned wary. "If it's about Mum, I'm not—"

Judith was through with beating about the bush. "Mum's going to call you later today."

"I'm not speaking to her."

Judith stood her ground. "What will it take for you to forgive her for last night?"

Pip scowled. "That was it, the final test. And she blew it big time."

By now Shaz had arrived on the sidelines. "Pip!" she said sharply.

"You need to stop this." She turned to Judith. "Anything you can do to get her to talk to your mum, I support."

Pippa gave Shaz a look that showed they'd obviously been talking—heatedly—about it all weekend.

"She was so rude to you," Pippa huffed, her face even redder than her hair. "She didn't acknowledge you as my partner, once."

"I don't care." Shaz stood her ground and glared at Pippa—quite fiercely, Judith thought. "If it takes her time to come around to us, so be it. After what you told me about her childhood, I get it. I really get it. You can't not talk to your mum; it eats you up inside."

"It's easy for you to say; your mum's the best," Pippa almost whined.

"And so is ours," Judith said firmly. "Mum always did her best. I know she got it wrong, I know she's never really understood you, but she loves you and she tries. She worried herself sick when she thought you had glandular fever, she drove you to netball, watched your matches twice a week, every single week. Went with you to all the weekend tournaments and stayed over, even though she hates being with lots of people."

Pip stared silently at the ground, unable to refute any of it, of course, because it was true.

"What would Mum have to do for you to forgive her?" Judith demanded again.

Pippa shrugged. "She'd have to say she totally accepts I'm gay and that Shaz and I are together. And not hang up when I—"

"Shout at her?"

"I only shout because she goes all weird and silent."

"You know shouting is hard for her, Pip."

"Well, it shouldn't be, she should just accept—"

Shaz put a hand up. "Okay, heard enough now." Pip stared at her. Shaz shook her head. "I love you, I absolutely love you, but sometimes you are such a stubborn cow."

Pippa's eyes rounded. "Cow! Did you just call me a cow?" She puffed out her chest and the two of them eyeballed each other. Then suddenly they both burst out laughing. Pip flung her arm around Shaz's shoulder and Shaz planted a kiss on her neck. "Urk, and a sweaty cow at that."

She made a gagging face, but her eyes were full of love as she gazed at Pippa.

"Fuck! Okay, okay, for you—and Jude—I'll talk to her. But I'll tell her it's only because you two made me."

"Don't you dare," said Judith and Shaz in unison.

Pippa traced patterns in the gravel with her foot, her lower lip jutting. A moment later her mouth quirked at the corners as she peered up at Judith. "Do you think I'm a stubborn cow, too?"

"Sometimes." Judith laughed. "But an adorable one."

"Egh. Couldn't you organise something?" Pippa wheedled. "It's so much easier to talk to Mum when you're there."

Judith fought the familiar tug in her chest. "No, Pip. I can't keep smoothing things out between you. You need to start talking to each other."

"It's so hard."

"Yes. It is. At first. But once you start, you'll find it gets easier. Just don't get shouty, okay?"

Pippa hung her head, and Shaz squeezed her shoulder. "C'mon, lover, you can do this."

"Okay. I'll count to ten and try to be non-shouty."

Shaz held up her other hand to Judith, who palmed it with hers.

"We've won."

As Judith walked away, she found she'd broken into a little jog.

Wow, wearing jeans, and laying down boundaries and falling in love all in one week was totally empowering.

CHAPTER 20

When Carts walked past Ron's office on Monday morning, he braced for the usual barrage of insults. He very much doubted that a week's leave would have improved Ron's warped view of the world. But a week *had* changed him. Beyond recognition.

He would no longer put up with Ron's shit.

All the way into the city he'd worked on a cutting, icily polite response that would put Ron firmly back in his box.

Head facing forward, spine erect, he stalked past his boss's door, and then... nothing.

No "Wells, wipe that hangdog look off your face" or "Got caught in a tornado on the way in, did you?" Not even the inevitable "Get a bloody haircut, boy!" even though now, of course, he'd had a miracle performed by the hair goddess, Tara.

When no spew of vitriol eventuated, Carts ground to a halt half a metre past Ron's door.

Curiosity made him step backwards and peer round the door.

The room was empty.

Ron may have outsourced his workload to the minions, but he was always at work earlier than everyone else. Ready to delegate while he drank coffee and chatted on the phone to one of his gnarly fishing mates.

Carts blinked at the sight.

Finally, he went to his desk in a bit of daze. As he powered up his computer, Travis's face popped over the partition and hissed, "Heard about Ron?"

Carts shook his head.

"He's being investigated."

"What for?"

"Harassment. Amy reported him for making constant derogatory comments about her appearance. And that's only the start I reckon."

"Fuck!"

"Yeah, apparently, that's why he wasn't here last week."

"Good on Amy," Carts said. It struck him that Ron had been cunning. He'd divided and conquered. Carts had always thought cheery Amy Nash with her can-do attitude had been a bit of a fave with Ron. He'd never heard a whisper that Ron was harassing her. But then, he'd never said a word about Ron's treatment of him either. Just hunkered down and tried to survive the onslaught.

Such was the power of bullies.

He got on with his day, feeling oddly fidgety, like a bullet had been removed from his gut, but still left an indent. At lunch time, it felt strange not to have to hurry back in case he got the usual barbed comments for being gone too long.

On a whim, he went and bought a gelato after he'd eaten his salad wrap.

Decisively, he ordered a scoop of cherry white chocolate and a scoop of salted caramel.

Then he strolled down to their secret spot, took a picture of the gelato and sent it to Judith.

Almost immediately, his phone pinged. *Awww yum. Wish I was there. Can't wait to see you tonight.*

They'd chatted on the phone yesterday evening for over an hour. She'd told him about her conversations with her mum and Pippa

"I don't know if they've talked yet. I kind of don't want to know," she'd told him. "I'm leaving it up to them."

"And if they don't, what then?"

There was a silence before she said, a little mischievously, "I won't make brownies for either of them, ever again. Come to think of it, I'm not sure I want to make brownies for *anyone* ever again."

He'd laughed. "Fancy meeting up tomorrow after work? Would that be—too keen?"

"No. I mean, yes, but no."

He'd frowned, and as if she'd felt it over the phone, she'd added, "Let's try again. No, it's not too keen and yes I'd love to."

So now the end of another day full of surprises was here, and he'd started to pack his things into his bag—phone, pens, water bottle—and was about to head for the exit when a voice behind him called out, "Carter. Can I see you for a moment?"

Shite. The big boss, Clive Pearson, no less.

"Come into my office, Carter."

Carts made his way to the other side of the eighth floor. Clive ushered him into his office and closed the door. When they were seated, Clive said, "I need to have a confidential chat with you, Carter."

Carts' collar tightened. Why did he still feel like there must be something he'd done wrong?

"Human resources are investigating a harassment claim against Ron," Clive explained. "Obviously the details are confidential, but I am asking everyone in his department to come forward with any other information about Ron's behaviour that might help us to get the full picture." He pinned Carts with a serious look. "Do you have anything you'd like to share? If so, I need you to make a time to meet with human resources."

Carts gave a slow nod. "I would like to speak to them. Yes."

Clive sighed. "I had a hunch you might. You know we don't stand for harassment at Pearson's. The problem we face is that often staff won't come forward and report their seniors for fear of recrimination. Thank you, Carter. I'll tell Alicia in HR to call you and make a time."

Carts got ready to leave.

"Another thing." Carts sat back down.

"We like your work. You are highly competent, and very well

thought of by your clients. We've had several of them phone us and praise you."

"Really?" Carts blinked.

"We asked Ron to pass that on at team meetings. Am I right in thinking he didn't?"

"I had no idea…"

Clive sat forward and steepled his fingers. "I've talked with the other partners, and while we're investigating this issue, we're in agreement we'd like you to step up. Act in the role of head of small business management."

Carts stared at a swirling blue glass paperweight on Clive's desk, trying to digest this information.

"Can I assume from your silence that's a yes?" Clive asked.

Carts looked up to see that he was smiling. "God yes. Thank you. I— I'm just—surprised." Completely gob-smacked would be more apt.

"You are one of our most valued employees," Clive said with genuine warmth.

A slow smile dawned. It seemed in the last seven days there had been a change in the weather, a deluge, washing away all that muddy shit from his past, leaving behind it a reservoir of clear water. A pool that reflected someone back to him that he could get to like and respect.

A guy called Carter Wells.

He wanted to air punch as he got in the lift. His only problem was that he was now running seriously late for Judith. She'd be arriving at his house any moment. He had to let her know what had happened.

He took his phone out of his briefcase. Tried to key in his PIN. Nothing happened. Tried again. The screen was totally unresponsive. Frozen to fuckery. Why now? He shook it, then turned it on and off. Christ, this served him right for putting off getting his cracked screen fixed.

What a stupid idiot.

And then he noticed them. The messages. Not on his phone, but inside his head, clear as if they were a text on his screen. "This always happens to you, doesn't it mate? Just as you think you've got your act together. Trouble is you're jinxed… Loser."

He saw that lonely kid in the playground, the constant insults scrolled on his locker, the dead stick insects hidden in his lunchbox, and the dry eucalypt leaves that replaced the ham in his sandwiches.

Enough. He closed his eyes, planted his feet wide, grounded himself and breathed deeply, in through his nostrils, out through his mouth.

He needed to let that picture go once and for all. It was redundant, broken like his phone.

When he opened his eyes, everything looked new, somehow brighter, shinier.

He exited the lift and headed for the train station.

He didn't panic when he saw the train leaving the platform, nor when the overhead screen said the next one would be half an hour.

He turned back the way he'd come and put one foot in front of the other.

Judith would wait for him.

Judith drew up outside Carts' house. When she'd been here for his birthday party a mere two weeks ago it had been dark, and she'd been so nervous that she'd barely noticed her surroundings. Now, curiosity took hold as she took a proper look. It was a neat, two-storey townhouse, part rendered and part coated in limestone that was the in thing right now. She should know, with all Dad's home designs.

Excitement mounted within her at the idea of going inside and finding out more about the man she was falling in love with.

She sucked in a breath. Yes. She could admit it now. This emotion that had fluttered in her heart since the moment their eyes first met. This was love. It made her feel like she was in one of those utterly romantic old movies, as if Carts was Humphrey Bogart to her Katharine Hepburn.

She wanted to wear fake furs and sit in a chic little bar and smoke Gauloises and drink fine white wine as rain fell on cobbled streets and Ultravox sang "Vienna" in the background.

With Carts, forever and always.

Smiling to herself, she was about to exit the car when she saw Solo bound out of the house, down the path and throw a leg over the red Ducati outside. He looked like a man with a mission. What were the bets he was off to see Polly?

After he'd driven off in a shower of exhaust fumes, she exited the car and made her way up to the front door.

Pressing the doorbell, she let her gaze roam around the tiny front yard. Neat succulents in pebble-mulched flower beds were laid out at meticulously spaced intervals. Now her inner domestic goddess replaced Katharine Hepburn. It could do with a few more flowers, some pansies and brightly coloured petunias maybe.

When he didn't answer, she guessed he wasn't home yet. Not to worry, trains could be delayed. She sat on the low front wall and waited. Crossed her legs. Uncrossed them. Got up and walked round the side of the house. Looked at the little splice of back lawn that was so neat she thought it must be fake, but when she bent down and ran her hands over it, found that it wasn't. Peering in the small shed, she saw some basic gardening stuff. A trowel, a bag of soil improver and a lawn-mower. It was kind of adorable thinking of Carts pushing it around his handkerchief-sized lawn.

Next, she peeped in the kitchen window. Everything was pristine. And completely devoid of anything that vaguely resembled a cooking implement.

Ten minutes had now passed, so she sent a quick message to Carts. *I'm here.* She went back around to the front of the house. Sat on the step and counted ants going in and out of a crack in a paver, and pulled out one lone weed from the path.

She checked her phone but there was no reply. And now, despite herself, she started to fret.

What if there'd been an accident? What if the train had smashed into a barrier? What if, as he'd crossed the road outside the station, in his excitement to reach her Carts had forgotten to glance over his shoulder as a truck hurtled towards him? Horrible images of finding the love of her life only to lose him had her eyes welling with tears.

Judith, this is silly, she told herself.

The panic started to turn her stomach to acid and sent icy fingers crawling up her spine.

But not for a single moment did she think he'd stand her up.

Finally, ten minutes later, having called him twice and sent three more messages, she called Polly.

"You haven't seen Carts, have you?"

"Was Carts home when you left?" she heard Polly say in response, obviously to Solo. Despite her fears, Judith had to smile.

"No, but let us know if he doesn't turn up."

"Okay."

She was just about to ring off when in the darkening light she saw a familiar figure getting closer by the moment, shoulders wide and his head held high. "It's okay," she told Polly, "he's here."

Joy and relief surged through her as she ran down the street and hurled herself into his arms.

Carts dropped his briefcase and embraced her. They stood in the street, hugging and kissing, as she told him she was worried he'd been in an awful accident. And he told her his phone had died. And they laughed and kind of almost cried, and that's when she said it.

"I love you."

Carts stilled. She felt the *thud, thud* of his heart against her chest. He buried his face in her neck and hauled in a shuddering breath.

Oh god, had she done it again? Got too enthusiastic? Said too much?

She tried to unwind her arms from around his neck and disentangle herself from his embrace. In response, he held her tighter, so her words when they came were muffled against his neck. "Maybe it's a bit too early to—"

"No!" Almost fiercely, he pulled back. Dark eyes held hers with vivid intensity before he gently sandwiched her cheeks with his palms. "Don't take it back."

Her heart stumbled, then started beating at double the rate.

"I love you too. I've been holding back saying it but every time I see you, touch you, kiss you, the words just want to come out. I know we've only known each other a few weeks, I know it's early days, I know all that. I know we've both been burnt by relationships, but this feels so

187

right. It *is* right. You and me, Judith. *We're* right for each other. I've known it from the first moment I saw you."

"Ohhhhhhhhh!" Now the tears welled over.

"I love you so much," he said. And then he kissed her mouth, tender at first, then bolder. Strong arms pulled her close, and his body pressed hard against hers, and the knowledge of his desire for her all came together, and a little sob of relief welled up in her chest.

After they'd kissed some more, he wiped the tears from her eyes.

"I hope these are happy." He dipped his finger along her lashes and caught one. She nodded and he said, "They're precious, like all of you."

She laughed shakily. "I imagined I'd lost you. Like those movies that look like they're going to end happily and then, suddenly one of them gets a terminal illness, or a tram runs them over or, or a meteorite crashes out of the sky, or..."

"Hey," he said. "I'm here, holding you tight, and loving you with every intact piece of me. See?" He waved a hand at the star-spangled sky. "No meteorite in sight. And outside of Adelaide and Melbourne, I think we're pretty safe from a tram incident."

Another shaky laugh as she burrowed back into him and they stood swaying together for a blissful moment as the news that HE LOVED HER AND SHE LOVED HIM sank deep inside her.

"I'm sorry," she sniffed.

"For what?"

"Crying. It's been a very intense week." A hiccup.

"I know," Carts replied. "Probably the most intense week of my life. And the best." They kissed some more, murmuring words of endearment.

Finally, Carts said, "Maybe we shouldn't stay out here, I think it's going to rain. Can I tempt you into my humble abode?"

"Said the spider to the fly."

He picked up his briefcase and they fell into step. "I've explored the outside," Judith said. "I found your lawnmower, and looked in the window. Your kitchen is very neat, and..."

"And?" He wrinkled his brow at her as he pulled out his keys.

"Empty."

He threw back his head and laughed. "I could probably locate a tin of baked beans."

"That sounds gourmet."

In the hallway, Carts hung her coat on a peg and led her past the living room. She spied the sofa with its carefully arranged cushions, a television, a coffee table, a turntable and a bookshelf full of all his LPs. She noticed a pot plant that was bright green and healthy looking. Carts saw where her eyes had travelled and said, "Plastic. Sorry."

In the kitchen he brought out glasses and a bottle of wine and opened the cupboard. As they shared the tin of baked beans (he hadn't been kidding, it was either that or a tin of spaghetti), Carts told her what had eventuated at work.

"So, you've effectively got a promotion."

"I'm only acting in the position. But, hey, I didn't even think Clive knew who I was... but there you are. Karma works, just like Fern says."

They drank the wine. Passed the tin of baked beans to each other. Cold baked beans were delicious when you were sharing them with the man you loved, Judith decided. Though she hoped there was a loaf of bread in the freezer because if she was going to stay the night, she'd need *something* for breakfast.

As if he read her mind, Carts said, "I've been doing a lot of soul searching. And I have to say I'm kind of ashamed that I can barely cook past boiling an egg and heating up takeaway food."

"And opening a can of beans?"

"That too. So, could you perhaps give me some lessons? You know, start simple. None of that baba good nosh stuff yet from what's his name."

"Ottolenghi."

His face lit up. "I could become the famous chef, Otto-leggy."

Judith slapped her forehead and rolled her eyes, then she came round, took the can from his hands and sat on his lap. "I meant it when I said I love your bad jokes. I'm also aware that love is blind." She pushed back the hair from his forehead and revelled in the caramel swirls in his dark eyes. "Now, changing the subject, does this house have a spa bath?"

189

He looked at her, a wicked grin shaping his lips. "No, but it has a really spacious shower. There's plenty of room for two."

She kept a straight face "That sounds—workable." And standing up, she took him by the hand.

"Lead the way, my gorgeous Otto."

Okay, so making love in the shower seemed like a great idea until Carts had knocked his head twice on the shower head and accidentally covered them both in a deluge of ice cold water trying to adjust the temperature. And when things had started to warm up again—literally *and* figuratively—he'd lifted Judith up (for obvious reasons) and she'd caught her butt on the tap while trying to wind her legs around him, they'd given up, and now lay naked on the bed, gazing deeply into each other's eyes.

It didn't matter.

Experimentation was something to approach with a lot of shared laughter and plenty of mutual respect.

Carts cupped her breasts, bent his head and kissed each of her nipples in turn, focusing on the smaller breast first, because as he pointed out, it needed to not feel inferior in any way. Then one thing led to another and on this occasion at least, the bed accommodated their needs perfectly.

A considerable time later, when they'd both got their breath back, Carts asked, "Where did you learn that trick?"

"Which one?" Judith asked lazily. Sex with Carts always seemed to make her really sleepy.

"The, er, tongue circling around the end of my..."

"From a little book I bought recently."

"I'm intrigued. Tell me more?"

She settled her head on his shoulder. "I found it at the Book Genie, it's called *Pleasure Your Partner,* by this sexologist called Dr Daphne Rubekind. It has all kinds of advice for how to communicate your needs, and um—positions, and... techniques."

"You'll have to let me look at it."

She giggled. "A bit of bedtime reading for both of us, maybe. To be honest, I'm not sure about all of her advice. I guess I've never really been into bondage, but she talks about it as a potentially playful, respectful kind of thing to tie your partner to the bedpost."

"And I do have an awful lot of ties in my closet."

She had an idea. "Maybe we could go through and make a list, cross off the ones that are definite nos then the maybes, and end up with the absolute must-dos."

"I have a better idea." He planted kisses along the line of her neck. "We could start with the must-dos, work our way to the maybes, and when we're lost for something to do on a dull rainy afternoon ten years from now, we could even explore the definite nos."

"I feel like I could spend the rest of my life with you focusing on the must-dos." She sighed happily.

They lay together contemplating the possibilities, until Judith's phone buzzed next to the bed. When she reached for it she smiled, and sat up against the headboard. "It's Mum. Listen to this: 'Talked to your sister. She didn't get shouty. It's a start.'"

Another message a moment later, Pippa this time.

"Talked to Mum. She apologised. I managed not to get shouty. It's a start."

Judith gave a rueful laugh. "They don't think they're alike. But they're just opposite sides of the same coin."

Carts was grinning at her. "Still feeling okay about not playing peacemaker?"

She tilted her chin. "Yes. I'll send a thumbs up and they'll be just fine without me. Besides, right now, I've got more pressing things to attend to." The phone messages seemed to have suddenly woken her up, and Carts' warm body next to hers was reminding her how many must-dos they had to work through. "Now, where were we..."

"I think we were about to try out the first of the must-dos. Dr Daphne Rubikscubes amazing strategy for simultaneous orgasms."

"No expectations or anything..."

"But practice makes perfect, right?"

Judith dived on him, laughing. "Absolutely!"

CHAPTER 21

*J*udith stood next to the Arrivals barrier at Perth International Airport, her hand clasped tightly in Carts'.

A full week had passed, and though not as eventful as the previous one, a lot seemed to have happened. Carts had started his new position as head of small business at Pearson's. He'd told her he'd brought his own chair in and put it behind Ron's desk because he couldn't hack the thought of his butt inhabiting the same spot as Ron's mouldy old arse.

Pippa had met Mum for a coffee and now apparently a meal was planned with Shaz and all four parents to meet and get to know each other. It was a coup of Herculean proportions, achieved with almost no input from Judith. She'd not heard a word from Mark. That was to be expected, but she had a plan to tackle that problem if the money wasn't in her account in a month.

As for her love life, well, she and her beloved had tried out at least a dozen more of the tips from *Pleasure Your Partner*, with plenty of check-ing, "is that okay for you? softer...? firmer...? maybe faster...? slower?"

Judith forced herself to focus on the imminent arrivals, not her blos-soming sex life.

"I think they're about to come through now," Carts said, craning his neck to see through the glass panel above the doors into the customs area.

Excitement swirled inside her, mixed with a little apprehension. What would she say when she met Aaron? And Alice? She really wanted to make a good impression.

A familiar heady perfume wafted past her nostrils and there was Polly, her curls wild around her face, wearing a checked 1950s style frock and high-heeled strappy sandals. Solo stood by her side, casual in black jeans and a black T-shirt.

Suddenly Judith felt like the plus one at a party where she wasn't really needed.

She found herself shrinking back a little, and immediately Carts seemed to sense it.

"What's the matter?"

She couldn't look at him. "You all know each other so well, and I'm the new girl on the block."

He ducked his head so she had to meet his eyes.

"And this is right where you belong." The non-negotiable tone in his voice sent a little quiver of desire through her. She loved when he played masterful. She resisted an overwhelming urge to nibble at his neck just below his ear.

Polly, who'd clearly been eavesdropping, looped an arm through Judith's. "You're stuck with all of us forever." So now judith found herself sandwiched between Polly and Carts. There were much worse places to be, she decided. "I want to be the one who introduces you to them," Polly said, popping her eyes at Carts in a challenge. "You were my friend before you met buggerlugs here."

"Stop muscling in on my girl," Carts teased back.

And then the automatic doors whooshed open and there were Alice and Aaron, pushing trolleys piled high with luggage. Judith had never met Aaron of course, but with his swept-back trendy blonde hair and bright blue eyes, she recognised him immediately from the photos.

As if surfing a wave, their little group surged forward, taking Judith with them.

Aaron suddenly spotted Carts and his face split into a huge grin.

He left his trolley by the barrier and, with a "Hey, mate!", locked Carts in a bear hug.

A lot of back-slapping took place and Judith tried not to feel a teeny-weeny spike of envy as with a squeal of "Munchkin!" Polly flew over to Alice and hugged her.

"Arghh, death by curls," Alice said, somewhat muffled by the barrage of Polly's hair, and everyone laughed. Now Polly hurled herself with almost the same enthusiasm at Aaron.

It reminded Judith of the way Pip hugged people; her whole being thrown into it, heart and soul.

Meanwhile, Alice had extricated herself from Polly's embrace and was heading towards Judith. In her jeans and red Converse, she only reached Judith's shoulder. "Hello, Judith." She smiled. "It's lovely to meet you properly."

To Judith's surprise, Alice went up on tippy toes, placed a hand on her shoulder and kissed her first on one cheek and then the other. "I've learnt the European way," she confided. "At first I'd get caught out when I didn't expect them to go for my other cheek, and we'd end up nose bumping, but I've got the hang of it now." Her dark eyes were warm behind her glasses and Judith realised why everyone loved Alice. She had a quiet way of making you feel special. An answering smile arced across her face. Alice reached up on tippy-toes again and murmured close to her ear, "He's a wonderful man."

"Yes, I can see that. Really very handsome," Judith agreed with a vigorous nod towards Aaron. Alice followed her gaze. "I didn't mean *him*. I do think Aaron is beautiful, of course—full of faults, and *so* vain about his hair, but I love him regardless. I meant Carts; he is the most kind, generous, beautiful man."

"I know." Judith felt her cheeks heating. "That's why I love *him*—well, one of the reasons."

Alice's eyes scrunched behind her glasses.

By now Polly was jiggling up and down in her Jimmy Choos. "So now I have to introduce you guys to my... my—what are you?" She cocked her head with a suggestive smirk at Solo.

"Your shrink?" he suggested. More greetings ensued, and firm hand-shakes were exchanged between Aaron and Solo.

"Well," Polly placed her hands on her hips, "now my two besties have finally met..." Judith blinked. Had she heard right? Did Polly really consider her a bestie? Her heart glowed as Polly continued, "Let's get out of here. I hate airports unless I'm the one flying off somewhere."

"We can't leave yet," Alice protested. "We've got to wait for Mum."

Polly's mouth formed a big O. "You mean Rowena's here too? Argghh, you never said."

"I didn't want to spoil the fun."

"Oh god." Polly rolled horrified eyes at Solo. "We're going to have to move out, babe."

Solo smirked and shot her an unmistakably lust-filled look.

"So where is she?" Polly craned her neck.

"Customs are probably checking out the binding on the books she's brought with her."

Aaron shook his head. "Rowena was in the row behind us and talked for hours to the guy next to her about some eighteenth-century feminist writer."

"Mary Wollstonecraft," Alice supplied.

He grinned lovingly at her. "Yeah, her. And your mum got louder and louder in direct correlation to how many gin and tonics she'd consumed. I'll take the screaming baby row any day over being stuck next to Rowena on a plane."

Alice slapped his arm.

A moment later all their eyes were drawn to a commotion at the automatic doors.

"Oh, golly gosh, I am so, *so* sorry."

A woman in an almost floor-length, brightly coloured silk dress, with tortoiseshell pins holding up a cascade of salt and pepper hair, stood looking helpless beside a completely empty trolley; the contents of which were now sprayed across the floor, blocking the exit.

Carts grinned. "Rowena Montgomery does it again."

"Oh Mum!" said Alice, rushing over to help. But before Alice reached her, a be-suited silver fox had started to pile Rowena's bags methodically back onto her trolley. Judith watched Rowena smile dazzlingly back at him.

"That's him," Aaron hissed, "the guy she was raving to on the plane."

"Oh James, you are *such* a gentleman, *thank you*." Now Rowena was batting her eyelids at the silver fox.

The man's gaze flashed obvious appreciation. "At your service. It was a pleasure to spend the flight with you—Rowena." He inclined his head before striding off into the crowd.

Rowena stood for a moment gazing wistfully after him. When she joined them, two dots of colour rode high on her cheeks. "What an absolute gentleman. Don't you just love the British?"

"Maybe you should have stayed there," Aaron remarked, lips twitching.

Rowena flapped a ring-covered hand at him. "Rude boy. And to think I have to put up with you as a son-in-law."

Then she spied Carts and, with a delighted exclamation, pitched towards him in a flurry of silk. "Carter!" She held him at arm's length. "Let me look at you. Goodness, I do believe you've grown."

"Haha. Funny—not." Grinning, Carts took Rowena by the elbow and led her over to Judith. "Rowena, I'd like to introduce you to my girl-friend, Judith."

"Lovely to meet you, Judith." Rowena appraised her with obvious admiration. "Where did you get such beautiful colour hair?"

"Oh, thank you." Judith pulled at a golden strand, not quite sure what to say. "I was born with it."

A moment later Dan barrelled like a missile into the midst of them and skidded to a halt, puffing from his sprint across the arrivals area. "Jesus Christ, the info board said the flight landed half an hour ago. Was it early?"

"No." Aaron laughed. "But Rowena got stuck in customs. Good to see you mate."

There followed more vigorous back slapping.

The warm glow around Judith's heart spread to the rest of her as she watched the exchange. How had it taken her until twenty-nine to find this wonderful group of people? Somehow they'd all inhabited the same city, walked the same streets, visited the same bookshop and never gotten to meet.

Gratitude filled her as Carts came and stood beside her.

"Happy?" he asked.

"Beyond happy," she said as she nestled her head onto his shoulder.

"Okay," said Aaron, like he was rallying the troops. "Forget the jetlag, let's all go to the Shamrock for a cleansing pint of Aussie Guinness. I've had enough of the Irish version. Anyone would think they invented it."

"I second that," said Dan.

"I third that," said Carts.

Carts' arms circled Judith's waist. As they walked towards the exit he bent his head and whispered in her ear, "The Shamrock, where it all began for you and me. Kind of fitting, isn't it? Like things have come full circle."

"Yes," she said as her gaze fell into his. "Like it was always meant to be." And it struck her that she was no longer that quiet, awkward, *tall* girl on the outside of the circle, looking in.

And Carts wasn't that quiet, awkward *tall* guy anymore, either.

They belonged right here, in the midst of their friends. And with each other.

A perfect circle of love.

EPILOGUE

One year later

Their party took up the whole of the second row of the St Catherine's College Auditorium.

Carts was seated on the aisle, because he knew his head was going to be in the way and it was quite feasible that someone would ask him to move. He had no problem with that, it was one of those facts of life.

Next to him sat Judith, then his mum and dad, Pippa and Shaz, then Kirsty and Luke, and finally, Judith's mum and dad. He looked around and saw Aaron, Alice, Polly and Solo in the row behind. Squeezing in late, of course, and disturbing everyone in the row, came Dan, muttering apologies.

Above the podium, big bubble cut-out shapes that could represent anything from hearts, to flowers, to abstract genitalia, hung on invisible threads.

NO NEVER MEANS YES.
MORE LOVE, LESS HATE.
MY BODY, MY RIGHT.

LOVE HAS NO GENDER.

And above them hung a huge rainbow with the words "THE RESPECT CONVENTION" arching across it.

A moment later Avery bounded onto the stage, a shiny saxophone in her hand. Her long legs were encased in black leggings and black patent lace-up boots below a short red kilt. A black beret was stuck at a jaunty angle over her dark hair.

Carts' heart swelled with pride.

She looked so confident, so stylish. So uniquely Avery.

With a little bow, she brought the saxophone to her lips. The opening bars of John Lennon's "Imagine" plunged the audience into rapt silence. Avery made that instrument weep as she swayed with the rhythm of the music.

She'd only been learning the sax for the past six months. How the heck did it seem like her and the instrument were one?

She was an amazing young woman, his sister.

When everyone applauded madly, Avery gave another bow in all directions, and then walked up to the microphone.

"As the Head Girl of St Catherine's College, it's my pleasure to open our first ever Respect Convention today. An afternoon of workshops for the pupils and families of St Catherine's College. We're here to celebrate our sexual diversity; to respect one another's differences, our similarities, and above all, our uniqueness."

Carts watched her draw in a breath before she continued, her dark eyes under her straight fringe scanning the audience.

"Last year I went to a party and got into a situation where a guy went further than I wanted him to. I said no. He didn't hear it as no. I froze in fear and if it hadn't been for my brother and his friend breaking that door down, it could have ended very differently. For a while there, I lost my way. I think I was trying to live up to some ideal of being 'accepted' and 'cool'. It took me a while to find my path back. As you can see, music is my passion, but so is equality. I'm still learning, still growing. I come from super tall genes so you know, I could end up 6 foot 6 like my brother… Where are you, Carts?"

She squinted into the lights. "Oh, yes, there he is, hard to miss." To

Carts' dismay, suddenly the spotlight was in his eyes. "Hi folks." He waved awkwardly, to another little ripple of applause.

"And yeah, once I was terrified of being tall, but now, hey I'm proud of the fact. Can't miss me, right?" An affirmative laugh from the audience."Later on, you'll hear from students who are straight, gay, transgender and non-binary, sharing their experiences openly and honestly. We'll hear from girls who've sent selfies of their naked bodies to boys and how it affected them when those posts went viral. We'll hear from boys who didn't know what they were supposed to do or say or how to behave on their first date. We're all here to learn, to understand and to respect one another's experiences. This is *our* time to be heard at *our* convention, put on by the year 11 and 12 students at St Catherine's College and supported by parents and staff." She stepped back, gave a funny little wriggle of her shoulders, and there for one second was the other Avery, the Avery who sometimes slept with her thumb in her mouth and Mutsy snuggled close.

There was room for both, Carts realised. Strength and vulnerability.

"So yeah," Avery cracked a huge grin, "Here we all are. Let the inaugural Respect Convention begin."

Thundering applause and statements of "Oh wow!" and "She's incredible" flew around the auditorium.

Judith squeezed his arm tightly, and he could see Mum wiping away a tear.

Pippa leaned forward from her seat and said, very loudly, "I want to be like Avery when I grow up."

MUCH LATER THAT AFTERNOON, Carts and Judith sat in their special spot down by the river. They'd come here often over the past few months after work, to chat and to watch the boats and just… be.

"That was the most incredible day," Judith said in awe. "Avery is a force to be reckoned with."

Carts laughed. "Did I mention she's decided to be prime minister one day? Jacinda Ardern has fired her up to go for the top job in Australia."

"Yay, Avery Wells for PM. She'd play the flute instead of making an inaugural speech and have the whole parliament in tears."

"The world needs more music. It would solve a lot of problems, I reckon," Carts said.

His phone beeped with a message. He looked at it and jumped up.

"I have to go."

Judith glanced up at him, confused. "What's happened?"

"Bit of an issue."

"Is everything okay? Nobody's hurt?"

"Everything's fine. But I have a job to do."

"But… but… I thought we were going to watch the sunset and then go for dinner with your family?"

"I'll be straight back. Promise." He bent down "I love you, by the way. Have I told you that today?" and kissed her.

She tried to grab his arm, but he slipped free and strode off. Perplexed, she watched his departing figure and then rubbed the little crease between her brows. She tried not to worry these days, but Carts was behaving strangely enough to make a girl concerned.

The next thing she knew, Polly and Alice had plonked down on either side of her on the bench.

"Hullo," said Polly. "Fancy finding you here."

"We thought we'd come and keep you company," said Alice, "until Carts gets back."

Judith looked from one to the other. "Oh, hi—so, you know where he's gone?"

Alice's face turned wooden. "Nope."

"Yes we do." Polly leaned forward and gave Alice a definite *look*. "There was an issue at work, wasn't there."

Judith looked from one to the other in disbelief. "It's Saturday."

"Well, you know, now Carts is officially the boss… always on call," Polly replied airily.

"No." Judith shook her head. "You're wrong. Carts believes in work/life balance. No-one in his team ever goes into the office on the weekend."

"Extenuating circumstances," Polly said with authority. Alice sniggered.

Judith fixed Polly with a hard stare. But Polly just kept gazing out to the horizon with a secretive little smile on her face. Next, Alice took out a bag of snacks and a bottle of champagne from the picnic bag at her side.

"You two are weirding me out." Judith shook her head. "Come on. Tell the truth!"

"Could you open this, Poll?" Alice passed the champagne across Judith. "You know I hate popping corks."

Judith caught sight of the label. "Veuve!"

Alice handed over a champagne flute. The cork made a satisfying pop and bubbles spilled into the glass.

"Are we celebrating something?" Judith asked as Polly handed her one and started pouring another. She tried to work out what might be going on. But Polly and Solo had got engaged six weeks ago and Alice and Aaron were going to be married next month, so unless it was a baby… but no, they wouldn't be quaffing champagne if that was the case, they'd be handing out mineral water.

"Diversity," Polly said with emphasis. "We're celebrating diversity."

"And respect," said Alice.

"And love," said Polly, and then, cocking her head to one side, she added, "Oh wait, Munchkin, can you hear music?"

"Probably a party boat." Alice sipped her champagne.

Polly gave a shrug. "Yeah, probably."

"Right, that's it." Judith attempted to get up. "I've had enough of this, French champagne or not. I'm going to find Carts."

A hand landed on her knee. "No!" This from Polly.

Another on her arm. "No!" echoed Alice. "Stay here."

Judith huffed and then her ears pricked. She knew that song, didn't she? The hauntingly beautiful lyrics floated across the water, making her goosebump all over.

Fields of Gold.

Pulse racing, Judith's gaze scanned the river. And then she saw it. Tacking at speed around the bend of the river—a streamlined yacht. Standing at the helm was a super tall guy. *Her* super tall guy. As it drew closer, she realised there were two other figures hauling up the third sail.

Aaron.

And Dan.

Only when that sail was fully unsheathed did Judith's mouth fall open and tears well up in her eyes. Words were scrolled in blue on the white sailcloth.

JUDITH, WILL YOU MARRY ME?

"Ohmygodohmygod!" She was cry laughing, her hands covering her mouth.

She looked from Polly to Alice, who were cry laughing too, and they both jumped up and down and then the three of them were squealing a whole heap of delighted jibberish.

As the vessel got closer to shore it was clear it was going to moor on the jetty.

Judith ran like she had the wind beneath her feet.

Carts stood on deck and pointed at his chest, and then at her hopping from foot to foot on the quay. He mouthed, "You? and Me?"

And she nodded and laughed until her head felt like it was going to fall off her shoulders.

As Aaron and Dan tied the ropes to the jetty posts, a crowd gathered. Carts jumped nimbly ashore and stood before her, all glorious six foot six and a half of him.

He went down on one bended knee. "Judith Mellors, will you marry me?"

"Yes, oh yes. Of course, I will," she managed between happy sobs.

A cheer went up from the assembled crowd.

The next moment more champagne was popping and, as if from nowhere, there were the rest of their friends and family. Pippa was suddenly hugging her fit to burst, then Shaz.

And behind them Judith saw the rest of her family and Carts' parents and Avery all smiling, laughing, crying too.

Carts' arms were around her waist. "I haven't bought the rings yet. I want us to choose them together."

She nodded, and then had to ask, "The boat... sailing....?"

"I've been taking lessons. With Dad."

She frowned. "So when you said you were playing squash...?"

"Yeah. Sorry. I know it was a little white lie, but for a really important cause."

"I forgive you."

"I thought maybe after we're married we could sail round the world. Just me and you," Carts said after she'd kissed him again.

Judith pulled a face. "I was thinking more of replanting the front yard. Maybe painting the front door."

"Nah, I figure a small six-foot catamaran, just room for two. And when it's stormy, we'll lock down in the hold, just me and you and..." Her face must have shown her horror, because he relented with a big grin. "Joke, my darling angel girl. This is the only place I want to be." One arm tightened around her and the other waved a hand at the little group marching towards them with purpose and beaming smiles. "With these friends. And most importantly, with you. *This* is my field of gold. I don't need wild adventures. You *are* my adventure."

"And you are mine," she murmured, her head resting against his shoulder.

Forget sailing the high seas, forget bungee jumping, forget navigating the South Pole on a husky-led sleigh.

This, here, with her handsome, big-hearted man by her side, was an adventure that would take the rest of her life to explore.

She was ready.

ALSO BY DAVINA STONE

The Alice Equation

The Polly Principle

THE FELICITY THEORY (AVAILABLE EARLY 2022)

When Oliver Blake's fiancé leaves him at the altar, his perfect world crumbles. So the very last thing Oliver needs at his brother's wedding three months later is a bubbly, red-headed bridesmaid plunging his life into more chaos.

Felicity Green has a theory—life is what you make it, and she's determined to make her trip to Australia one hell of an adventure.

Somehow Oliver finds himself heading across Australia with Felicity in an old combi van, and before long it's obvious they're both carrying excess baggage. As they share confined travel arrangements and starry outback nights, secrets from their pasts emerge.

Soon things are heating up, and it has very little to do with the Australian sun!

On reaching Sydney it seems Oliver and Felicity have found something strangely perfect, until a hurdle arises that just might be too big for either of them to overcome.

Will Felicity and Oliver find a way through this, or has their journey into love reached the end of an outback road?

ABOUT THE AUTHOR

Davina Stone writes romances about flawed but lovable characters who get it horribly wrong before they finally get it right. They also kiss a fair bit on the way to happily ever after.

Davina is a proud Anglo-Aussie having lived half her life in both countries. When not writing she can be found chasing kangaroos off her veggie patch, dodging snakes and even staring down the odd crocodile. But despite her many adventures, in her heart, she still believes that a nice cup of tea fixes most problems—and of course, that true love conquers all.

Please Review This book.

Reviews help authors to keep writing and help readers to find our books. If you enjoyed *A Kiss For Carter*, please consider leaving a review on your preferred platform.

Why not drop by and say hi?

Want to read the story of when Alice and Aaron first met? Sign up for my newsletter (available on my website) and get the prequel to the first in the Laws of Love series, *The Alice Equation* FREE. You will also get updates on new releases and regular bonus reads exclusive to my newsletter.

Check out my website at https://www.davinastone.com/ and connect with me on